T0165517

The white witch and the curse of...

THE PINK SALAMANDER

The white witch and the curse of...

THE PINK SALAMANDER

by

Gordon Yates

authorHOUSE®

AuthorHouse™
1663 Liberty Drive
Bloomington, IN 47403
www.authorhouse.com
Phone: 1-800-839-8640

© 2013 by Gordon Yates. All rights reserved.

No part of this book may be reproduced, stored in a retrieval system, or transmitted
by any means without the written permission of the author.

Published by AuthorHouse   03/06/2013

ISBN: 978-1-4817-8329-3 (sc)
ISBN: 978-1-4817-8330-9 (e)

Any people depicted in stock imagery provided by Thinkstock are models,
and such images are being used for illustrative purposes only.
Certain stock imagery © Thinkstock.

This book is printed on acid-free paper.

Because of the dynamic nature of the Internet, any web addresses or links
contained in this book may have changed since publication and may no longer be
valid. The views expressed in this work are solely those of the author and do not
necessarily reflect the views of the publisher, and the publisher hereby disclaims
any responsibility for them.

CHAPTER 1

———————— •●• ————————

Dan Kovak's thin, jug shaped face was creased in an expression of incredulity as he re-examined the photograph on his computer. He had read the brief report that accompanied the photograph but that offered no satisfactory explanation for the anomaly. His free hand went automatically to the tuft of reddish hair perched on his head and smoothed it down in frustration.

'How can this be?' he muttered to himself. 'It doesn't make sense.'

He was looking at the output of the CIA's satellite, nuclear activity surveillance system, with his nose almost touching the computer screen.

'Put your proper specs on Dan, then it might look better.' The voice came from the other side of the desk partition. Dan waved a dismissive hand at the remark. 'Come and look at this Will.' he said in an excited, high pitched squeak.

Will Gorman manoeuvred his bulk around the partition and flopped onto Dan's desk. Dan ruffled his hair as though to emphasise the Laurel and Hardy tag the pair had collected from their colleagues.

'Have you ever seen anything like this before?'

On his screen was a satellite image of a north London street at night. One particular house was bathed in a strange, iridescent, glow.

'What's the radiation spectrometer say?' said Will, shifting his position to get a better view. The desk creaked alarmingly as he leaned across Dan and poked a chubby finger at the keyboard.

'There's no radiation but there are some products of a nuclear reaction.'

'A nuclear reaction?' they chimed together.

'Naw! That can't be right,' said Will. 'There's been a nuclear reaction in a boring suburb of London? Either your machine's unserviceable or the satellite's telling lies.'

'I did a self test on the satellite and it's functioning ok,' said Dan. 'Check it out on yours.'

Will waddled around the partition and regained his own seat. Thirty seconds later he gave a low whistle. 'My God it's right,' he said, 'some sort of nuclear reaction; but how can that be? How come it's so localised? It's only around that one house; everything else seems to be unaffected. Go on Google, see what that freaky house is and who owns it. How old is that report?'

'Almost a year,' said Dan.

'So why has it only just been picked up?'

'Well, I suppose among the thousands of minor conflagrations round the world it could be rated insignificant; that is, until you analyse it.'

'Unless of course, it's been deliberately suppressed.'

Will rolled his eyes in the direction of the department head's office.

'Now why would anyone want to do that?' chuckled Dan ironically. 'Everything's so transparent in this organisation.'

'It wouldn't be the first time,' muttered Will. 'Even the "john's" regulated by political correctness these days.'

Dan chuckled and the two men fell into silence, punctuated only by the clacking of Dan's keyboard as he searched the zip code information. He gave a whoop of success. 'The house belongs to a Chinese guy called Chu and he has a daughter called Lucy.'

'Ah! Chu,' said Will.

'Bless you!' giggled Dan in his falsetto voice.

'So what kind of food are they cooking in that takeaway; wanmegaton soup?'

'Dunno,' chuckled Dan. 'Peking duck with extra quark perhaps, but I think we ought to find out, don't you? Ah! It says here that he's a physicist normally based at Shanghai University.'

'So why is he in England?' asked Will.

'He isn't, he's been deported.'

'And his daughter?'

'Now there's another mystery,' said Dan. 'According to their police, she's English and they deported her at the same time as her father.'

'Why would they deport one of their own citizens?'

'Search me; she must have been extremely naughty. None of this makes sense. It goes on to say "she no longer exists", whatever that means. Not dead but, "no longer exists!"'

'OK, so let's prove 'em wrong,' said Will, typing Lucy Chu into the find feature of the National Security Agency's supercomputer.

. . . .

Lucy opened her almond shaped eyes and surveyed her surroundings. She had found it difficult to adjust to the confines of a student room on the Liverpool University campus after having the freedom of the whole house at fourteen Lichfield Crescent. That of course was now uninhabitable and there was no going back there. Her father was right; she had to disappear after what had happened. In fact, the whole teleportation experiment had been suspended. A year had passed without incident or excitement, and she had settled down to the rigours of academic life with determination and enthusiasm. Chu's ploy appeared to be working and any police hue and cry for the elusive Chinese looking, Lucy Chu, had faded away.

A year ago she had emerged, blinking, into the glare of early morning winter sunshine, from Lime Street Station. The journey from Euston had been uneventful but as her father had pointed out, necessary in view of the previous evening's catastrophic events. They had stood together in what used to be the bedroom of Chu's north London house and surveyed the damage. This room had taken the full force of the onslaught and was clearly no longer safe. The rest of the house had fared little better. The terraced houses on either side were strangely, completely untouched by the grinding, screeching earthquake, shattering high velocity winds and fierce electric storm that had occurred. Chu knew the neighbours would be clamouring for explanations and shortly involving the police and media. He realised he must be quickly transported back to China and his daughter must find a safe, anonymous location, far away from the aftermath of the battle with the forces of evil.

As for Jack and Megan, it was better that they did not know of Lucy's whereabouts as they were sure to be questioned by the ever inquisitive D.I. Livingstone and his colleague, D.C. Collins. Chu had made two short phone calls, pushed a piece of paper into her hand and then, with her help, disappeared through the portal back to China. Lucy had grabbed her meagre belongings stuffed them into her backpack along with her all important laptop, climbed into the taxi ordered by Chu and had set off to Euston station. When safely on the train she had unfolded the piece of paper and read her instructions. Chu had anticipated something like this happening and had planned her escape and subsequent disappearance meticulously.

The note read: "Lucy, there are those who would destroy our work and possibly ourselves, because of the fear of that which they do not understand. Please take the following precautions while maintaining the possibility of continuing our activities. Take the train to Liverpool and present yourself at the university to a Mr Gregory Harness, who is head of the physics faculty. Gregory has been partly responsible for setting up a new university in partnership with Xi'an Jiaotong based in Suzhou Industrial Park, near Shanghai. I know him well and I can assure you that he is trustworthy. I previously arranged with him that he would look after you should the circumstances arise. He knows nothing of our work, however, and that is how it should remain in order to protect him, as much as ourselves. He will enrol you in the three year physics degree course as a special entry and arrange for your accommodation on campus. Do not concern yourself with the cost; that has all been arranged. I think you will find Liverpool an ideal place to become anonymous as there is a large Chinese community not far from the university. Please do not attract attention to yourself and try to be patient. The time will come when we will be able to unveil our findings to the world without fear of reprisals; it is just not that time yet. Stay in touch with me, and by all means your friends, Jack and Megan, but always encrypt any emails and do not let them know where you are. Be careful, your loving father."

She had read and re-read the instructions which were, for him, uncharacteristically terse, and concluded that he was under pressure to maintain complete secrecy, suggesting that even the Chinese government was not fully aware of the radical new science he had discovered. She had obeyed his instructions to the letter, with the desired result. She had faded into the Chinese community of Liverpool and was now, just one more nondescript Chinese face among thousands inhabiting the Chinatown area.

She knew Chu was continuing with the work, but realising the danger it represented to her, he no longer involved her in the practicalities of matter transportation. As for her erstwhile colleagues, Jack and Megan, they were both at university in Cambridge and were better left to continue their studies in peace. Now with at least two meals a day and a comfortable bed, she had allowed her strict regime of self control to diminish. Saturday morning was for any person her age, a time for lying in bed and reflecting on life in general and her own situation in particular.

She glanced at the clock on her bedside locker. *Mmm, time to get up.* She swung her legs out of bed and switched on her laptop. Crip appeared after a short delay and stood on top of the laptop screen. 'Rucie, you have email from last night,' he beamed.

'Thanks Crip,' she murmured drowsily, and opened her inbox.

The paper clip, a bizarre by-product of Chu's science, bowed from the waist with a big grin splitting his bent metal face.

Lucy was startled. 'Are you alright Crip?' she remarked.

'I been learning etiqu . . . etiqu . . .'

'Etiquette.' Lucy finished the sentence for him.

'That light,' he agreed. 'From Dunnit, I going to be proper English, like you Rucie.'

'I'm so glad to see you two are getting on well together,' she said as she read the message from Donna, the Liverpudlian girl occupying the room across the corridor.

"Hi Jude," she read, "get yer glad rags on tonight, 'cos we're wavin' a wicked welly at the "Krazyhorse". See ya! P.S. tried to phone you about it last week but you didn't reply. I'da thought somebody doin' physics would know how to use a phone."

Crip, seeing Lucy's reaction to this said, 'You no wanna go Rucie?'

'S'pose I shall have to conform,' she said, typing a quick response.

'You want herp with clothes,' said Crip opening a local dress shop website on screen.

She shuddered with displeasure, sprang to her feet, and opened her wardrobe door to reveal the minimal amount of clothes in there. One pair of shabby trainers, one baggy jumper, a fleece for winter wear, a red shell suit, one pair of flat shoes, her old school uniform, two pairs of jeans and the black cocktail dress her mother had given to her after the divorce. She stroked the sleeve of the dress and briefly remembered the pain of her parent's separation. She hadn't seen, or contacted Carla, her mother, since she and Jack had been in The Hague a year ago. That was necessary, for any conversation would be passed to Albert, her current partner, and he was not to be trusted. This was not because he wasn't respectable, or likeable, but simply because of the nature of his employment. His job, as an exploration engineer at Shell in the Hague was to assist in the production of oil and its products and Chu's science would eventually remove the necessity for that, at least where used for transport. Of course he would be interested if he knew the technology had been advanced to the point at which teleportation of matter was now possible. His future relied upon it being impossible!

She took the cocktail dress out of the wardrobe and slipped it on then examined the result critically in the full length mirror attached to the wardrobe door.

'Velly nice Rucie,' said Crip, helpfully.

The dress hung limply on her slight figure and was clearly one size too large. 'Oh I don't know what to do Crip, this just isn't me,' she said woefully. 'I don't seem to be able to fit in with this lifestyle.'

Later that morning there was a hammering on her door. As Lucy opened it, Donna almost fell into the room, shrieking with laughter.

'C'mon!' she yelled, 'We're goin' shoppin'!'

'What for?'

''Cos yer neva gona get a fella lookin' like that.'

'Looking like what?' countered Lucy, feeling slightly insulted.

'I think those rags have grown on yer,' said Donna, pointing at her jumper. 'We need to get yer tarted up Jude.'

. . . .

Lucy gazed longingly at her clothes which were lying in a tangled heap on the changing room floor while Donna chattered on incessantly.

'You'll be really made up when I've finished with yer,' she was saying.

Lucy wasn't listening. She was already regretting having agreed to go out to the local nightclub later.

'But I haven't anything suitable to wear,' she had protested.

Rather than seeing this as a possible excuse, Donna had relished the opportunity to go shopping and exercise her fashion skills on this unwilling subject. Lucy had relented and agreed to make the effort when she remembered that her father wanted her to blend into the background of college life. It was now with something approaching despair that she surveyed the reflection confronting her in the full length mirror in the dress shop changing room.

'I'm not sure about the shoes,' she said, 'they seem awfully high.'

She tottered around in a circle to emphasise the point.

Donna screwed up her nose, 'Well that's the fashion now, no use gett'n a cob on. You have to suffer a bit if yer going to be fashionable. But yer'll have to get those leggings off; yer'll be far too hot when you're dancin'.'

'Dancing?' A look of terror crossed her pretty face and her almond eyes widened. 'Must I?'

'Definitely!' Donna said, tugging at the waistband.

Lucy obligingly slipped off her black leggings to reveal the almost faded scars from her battle with the demons at number fourteen Lichfield Crescent.

'Oh my God,' exclaimed Donna, 'which divvy did that?'

'Dogs,' said Lucy dismissively.

Assuming no further explanation was forthcoming, Donna continued to dress and undress her victim until she was satisfied with the result. 'There,' she said finally, with obvious pride, 'who's a pretty Judy then?'

Lucy had to admit the transformation was incredible. She had never in her twenty years dressed like this before. For the first time she felt like a woman and although not admitting it openly, she liked it.

'Now to accessorise,' crowed Donna.

After a further hour of bags, baubles and beads, Lucy was allowed to escape once more into her baggy jumper, leggings and shabby trainers.

'I'll call for you at eight,' was Donna's parting shot. 'We need a bevvy before we go onto the club.'

'But I don't drink,' protested Lucy.

'God you're a sad human being,' twinkled Donna happily, 'so you'll just have to learn won't yer?'

. . . .

CHAPTER 2

Albert had stood in front of what used to be number 14 Lichfield Crescent in a state of mild shock because there was no sign of the house, unless the gap where it had been could be counted as a sign. As she had not heard from Lucy for almost a year Carla had asked him to check she was okay while he was on business at the Shell Centre in London. Albert had no interest in Lucy's welfare. He was not her stepfather and did not plan to become committed in that way. However, he had readily agreed in order to satisfy his own suspicions concerning the nature of the experiments conducted by her ex husband and Lucy. Now he stood in the space where Chu and Carla's house had been, intrigued as to what had caused the house to be demolished.

'Interesting,' he murmured to himself. 'I think a visit to the neighbours might provide some answers.'

The house to the left was unoccupied, a "for sale" sign hanging precariously from its brickwork, fluttering in the gusting breeze. He knocked on the door of the house on the right. A grey haired, bespectacled old man opened the door.

'Ja! Excuse me,' said Albert. 'I am enquiring after the previous occupants of the house which used to be next door.' He gestured at the gap in the row. 'Do you know what happened to them?'

'Now there was a funny thing,' the man began, leaning forward conspiratorially, 'you ain't gonna believe this. Are you a relation then? Come in; fancy a cuppa tea?'

'Sort of. My name's Albert. The young Chinese looking girl who used to live there, I'm her mother's partner. Her mother's very concerned about her whereabouts.'

'Well it's all very mysterious.' said the man, ushering Albert through into his sitting room. 'You're the second one today. It's like buses . . . none for a year, then two come along at once.'

'This first man,' said Albert, thinking quickly, 'may have been a friend of mine, could you describe him?'

'Not a *him* mate, a *her*, with legs up to her armpits.' His eyes twinkled and his face creased into a leer at the memory. 'Very nice piece of crumpet,' he mused.

'So what did she want?'

'Pretty much the same thing as you. She was enquiring after the girl. Lucy, I think she called her.'

'Ja! That's her,' agreed Albert. 'Do you know where she went? Did she leave a forwarding address?'

'No, I kept meself to meself, what with all the comings an' goings in there.' He nodded in the direction of the gap.

'Comings and goings?' asked Albert. 'What sort of things went on in there?'

'Strange, blue flickering lights coming from the conservatory. Shouting and wailings fit to make yer blood go cold. Police were in an out of that house like a fiddler's elbow. Not that they ever found anything.' The old man's face became wild and staring as he recalled the incidents. 'Then on the last night, the night the house was wrecked, came this visitation from the other side. Devils were running about; howling winds, screaming and flashing blue lights, like an electric storm. Then earthquakes and the whole street shook as though it was all going to fall down. Suddenly it stopped . . . nothing, like someone had turned off a switch. There was more than one person in the house, I could here them talking. I think they all escaped unharmed. At least the police didn't find any bodies, but I've no idea where they went.'

'Did you see any of the people leave?'

'You must be joking mate. I wasn't going to stick my nose into that business. I was hiding in the backroom, well out of the way until things calmed down. Strange thing was though, from the power of it, you'd have expected half the street to be demolished, but no, just next door copped it, nothing else.'

'Was it reported in the newspapers?'

'Oh yus!' replied the man. He glanced slyly at Albert. 'I've got a cutting somewhere upstairs; I'll go and get it.'

He made his way upstairs. Pausing on the landing he pulled a mobile phone from his pocket wrapped in a crumpled fifty pound note. Holding the banknote in one hand he dialled the number scrawled on the back of it with the other. He moved into his front bedroom and looked out of the window.

'Yes,' he whispered into the mouthpiece, 'there's a man 'ere called Albert, he's tall and blond. I think it's his hire car parked in front of my house.'

There was a pause, and he then quoted the registration number of the car standing in the street below.

'Same deal?' he whispered. 'In an envelope through the letter box? Good on yer lady.'

Retrieving the press cutting from a bedside drawer, he went downstairs and handed it to Albert. Albert scanned it briefly. There was no explanation given and it was clear that the police had no idea what had caused the damage, but it did mention by name the police officer conducting the investigation; Detective Inspector Livingstone.

'This woman who came to see you, was she from the police?'

'Aw no mate, she wasn't a blue bottle; no way. You can tell those bastards a mile off from the way they talk, all robot like, as though they're reading a script. Naw, she might have been from the council though.'

'When was she here?'

'Late yesterday.'

Albert's face creased into a worried frown. Who else could possibly be interested in the whereabouts of Lucy Chu? He thanked the man for his help and placed a ten pound note in his outstretched hand as he left.

Back at his hotel room Albert did a quick search of the local telephone directory. After a few false starts he located the ex D.I. Livingstone, and arranged to see him that afternoon.

. . . .

Chief Superintendent Joan Wiley shifted uneasily in her chair and turned over the House of Commons headed letter she had just received. Her frown deepened as she re-read the terse instruction; "China and America have no extradition treaty, it is therefore incumbent upon your department, on behalf of America, to detain Mr Chu and his daughter should they appear in your area of responsibility. We are aware that Mr Chu has previously entered this country illegally and should therefore be arrested for questioning at the first opportunity as he may pose a terrorist threat."

She chose to ignore the rest of the letter, it being mainly concerned with the dubious legalities of America's use of extraordinary rendition.

'Why America?' she murmured. 'Why are *they* interested in a problem we had deporting a Chinese national?'

She slumped back in her chair, her eyes narrowed in an expression of intense concentration, as she tried to remember the details of the very puzzling case of Mr Chu and his daughter, Lucy. Finally she picked up the phone.

'D.S. Collins? My office, now!' she barked.

There was a shuffling of feet outside the door and a hesitant knock.

'Enter!'

Another hesitant knock.

'Come in!' shouted C.S. Wiley, her frustration mounting.

The door creaked open and the red faced, red haired Collins appeared, a startled expression on his face.

'First of all I suppose I should offer my congratulations on your promotion,' she began.

The face went a shade redder.

'You were involved in the unfortunate case of the Chinese girl who kept disappearing and the deporting of her father back to China were you not?'

'Yes Ma'am.'

'Along with D.I. Livingstone, who is no longer with us?'

'Yes Ma'am.'

'I want you to get the file and yourself back to this office immediately.'

'Yes Ma'am.'

Five minutes later Collins re-appeared with a rueful expression, but empty handed.

'File!' said C.S. Wiley, holding out an expectant hand.

'Sorry Ma'am, it seems to be missing.'

She fixed him with an icy stare. 'Nonsense!' she snapped, 'Nothing goes missing in my department without my permission.'

By and large this was true, with the possible exception of D.I. Livingstone, whose nervous breakdown and subsequent incarceration in a mental institution, was entirely unforeseen by the formidable C.S. Wiley.

'I presume you filed all data, reports etcetera at the time of the case?'

'Yes Ma'am, D.I. Livingstone was very careful to make sure everything was recorded and filed.'

'So how is he?'

'Not good Ma'am. I don't think he enjoys early retirement and he is still troubled by what happened.'

'As apparently are we, particularly when we are incapable of maintaining our records. I suggest you use your detective skills and find that file Collins . . . now!'

. . . .

When Albert introduced himself as Keith Jenkins, a journalist investigating possible paranormal happenings, Livingstone's haggard, vacant expression was transformed into one of animated interest. When Albert said he was specifically interested in the strange case of Lucy Chu, he became quite excited, so much so, his wife had to calm him down.

'How did you here about it?' said Livingstone, guiding Albert through into his small lounge.

Albert produced the newspaper cutting.

'Ah! I see,' said Livingstone. 'Well of course that's only a very small part of the story.'

'Do you think you should keep going over all this?' interjected his wife, with a worried frown. 'You know he's only just come out of hospital,' she directed at Albert.

'But this man is a psychic investigator dear, he can help me solve the mystery and then maybe I can get my job back,' protested Livingstone, eagerly.

'All right,' she said kindly. 'Just don't expect too much. I'll go and make a brew. Will tea be alright Mr Jenkins?'

Albert nodded. 'You said that's only a small part of the story,' he coaxed, gently.

'Oh yes I've got the complete story here,' he said opening a drawer in a small bureau and pulling out a buff coloured file. 'I've been working on it for months.'

'Working on it?' queried Albert.

'Yes, if I can find out how these things were happening,' he patted the file, 'I can maybe convince my boss that I'm not insane and I can have my job back.'

'What sort of things were happening that led your boss to believe you were . . . insane?'

'Lucy Chu was able to disappear at will. She did this from a locked police interview room with a policewoman present. At one point she was murdered, I saw her body myself, and then she re-appeared. Of course no one would believe me.'

'How strange,' said Albert thoughtfully. 'You've no idea how she did these things?'

'The only clue I had was her computer. Now I know nothing about computers, Mr Jenkins, but when it was examined by the police forensic department they said there were certain parts of it which they couldn't access, even with the DVD.'

'DVD?'

'Oh! Yes. There was a DVD which seemed to be in Chinese, but we drew a blank there also. It's all in here,' he said handing the folder to Albert.

Albert glanced through the folder and noted that it was a police file. He concluded that it should not really be in Livingstone's possession. 'May I take this away to study it in more detail?' he ventured.

'Oh well I don't know . . . I'm not supposed to have it you see, I borrowed it for a while and I shall have to return it sometime.'

'Would you to loan it to me, say for two hundred pounds, so that I can help you get to the bottom of this?'

'You wouldn't print the story would you?'

'Not without your permission Mr Livingstone, but we would pay you handsomely if you were to agree to it.'

Livingstone's wife appeared from the kitchen carrying a pot of tea and spotted the police file. 'Oh good,' she said, 'you're getting rid of that thing. I'm sick of the sight of it. It was making you worse. I don't think you should have it anyway.'

'I think you're very wise Mrs. Livingstone,' said Albert as she handed him a cup of tea. 'I shall attempt to get to the bottom of this on your behalf and your husband can stop worrying about it. When I have an answer, I will be in touch. I have your telephone number.' He placed four fifty pound notes on the coffee table and picked up the file.

'Which magazine do you work for Mr Jenkins?' she said.

'Oh I'm freelance,' he replied, 'I will sell the article where we will get the best price and you will get the most benefit.'

As he left the house, he failed to notice another hire car parked further along the road. The occupant, however, did not fail to notice that Albert was carrying a file under his arm which he had not carried *into* the house earlier.

CHAPTER 3

— •◦• —

Later that evening, Albert spent some time in his hotel room, looking through the police file he had just bought from Livingstone. The contents confirmed his suspicions that Lucy and her father had succeeded in transforming matter into energy and teleporting the result, although there was no direct reference to this. He didn't expect there to be, after all this was a police file and they dealt only with facts, not conjecture. Disappearing bodies was the key to it all; they just didn't melt away in the morgue in any other way. He decided there and then that he had to find out how it was done. He reasoned that whoever could apply this science had immense power which could be used for personal gain . . . his personal gain. The ability to roam anywhere while remaining out of reach of any authority was amply demonstrated in the police report and greatly appealed to him. This is what Lucy, and presumably Chu also, could do, and he now wanted it badly. The police report identified only one thing of note in the house and that was a computer and an associated DVD, as described by Livingstone earlier. *So,* thought Albert, *this is the key to it. Whatever is on that DVD is the answer and wherever Lucy is, she must have that disc with her; find Lucy, find the disc; simple!* The other piece of information contained in the file was Lucy's mobile phone number. It would seem the police, on one of their visits to the house had come across the phone and made a note of its number on the off chance that it could be used to track her down. In this, the police had drawn another blank as Lucy had never used the phone at all. 'Still,' mused Albert, 'it's worth a try.' He rang the number and after accessing the voice mail account, was greeted by a young woman's voice, which was not Lucy's. It was a message from someone called Donna, telling Lucy that a group of girls were going out to the "Krazyhorse" nightclub the following weekend and that Lucy would be going with them. He concluded that as the message had not been deleted, Lucy had never read it. He pondered for a long time over the accent of the girl and why she referred to Lucy as "Jude." Not being a native speaker, English accents were alien to him, and although it felt like a clue, he had no way of resolving it. Suddenly he had an idea and putting his phone in his pocket; he carefully placed the file in the bedside cabinet and went down to the hotel reception desk.

The receptionist looked up as Albert approached. 'Yes sir, can I help you?'

'Ja, you may be able to,' said Albert. 'Can you listen to this message and tell what part of England the young lady comes from?'

'I'll give it a try,' said the receptionist, looking intrigued. He concentrated hard for a few seconds then handed the phone back to Albert. 'Scouse!' he proclaimed, emphatically. Albert looked at him blankly and shook his head. 'Scouse!' repeated the receptionist; then realising that Albert was no wiser for this said; 'Liverpool!'

'Ah!' said Albert, 'Are you sure?'

'Certainly! I come from Blackburn; she's definitely a Liverpudlian.'

'Liverpool University,' whispered Albert to himself, 'so that's where she is. Tell me why does she call the recipient 'Jude' when her name is Lucy?'

'Ah! Well that's probably a bit of folk lore dating back to the Beatles. "Hey Jude!" Remember? "Jude", short for Judy, became a generic term for any woman after that song. Well that's my theory, for what it's worth. Of course I wasn't even born then, so I could have got that wrong. Anyway, she's definitely a Scouser.'

'Well thanks for that, and the education,' said Albert.

He picked up the drink he had ordered and made for a quiet corner of the bar where he could do some thinking. Pulling out a small notebook and a pencil from his pocket, he began to make sketches and notes, until an attractive brunette interrupted his deliberations.

'May I sit here?' she said, occupying a chair and giving him no opportunity to refuse.

'Yes of course,' he said, putting away the notebook with an admiring glance at his guest.

He looked around the bar. It was early and only occupied by a few people.

'Are you on business?' she said offering her hand, 'I'm Jane.'

'Yes,' he replied gently shaking her hand, 'I'm Albert.'

'So, Albert, what do you do for a living?' she said smoothly in her American accent.

'I work for Shell in The Hague, and you?' he said, trying not to sound too pompous.

'Oh nothing so grand, I work for a personnel recruitment agency.' She noted his raised eyebrows, 'I cast my net and look for exceptional talent.'

'Have you caught any good fish today?' he joked.

'Not yet but I'm still angling . . . why, are you interested in being recruited?'

'I may be,' he said. 'Can I buy you a drink?'

'Vodka tonic,' she replied.

Albert walked up to the bar and while ordering drinks engaged the barman in conversation once more. 'Do you know that lady . . . is she a guest?' he said motioning towards her with his eyes.

'Yes sir, I checked her in myself earlier this afternoon.'

'Thanks!' said Albert, 'Have a drink on me.' He slipped a ten pound note over the counter. The barman pocketed the note with a grateful smile and went back to polishing glasses.

Albert resumed his seat. 'What sort of people do you recruit?' he said, feigning interest.

'I do a good line in male models.'

'What attributes are you looking for?'

'I prefer men who are thirty-ish, tall and blond.'

Albert could feel himself being sucked in but didn't have the strength to resist this charming, elegant woman.

'Are men like that better suited for showing off clothes?'

'Did I mention clothes?' she said with an alluring smile. 'You're not English are you?'

'No, Dutch.'

'I find English men very restrained,' she said languidly, 'almost as if their wives are looking over their shoulders all the time.'

'And the unmarried ones?'

'They're mostly insecure for one reason or another and I don't have the time or energy to unravel their puerile hang ups. You're not married are you Albert?'

'Good heavens no!'

Albert felt the shake of his head was maybe a little too emphatic, and decided to employ a little more English restraint henceforth. *Although* he thought, *she is extremely desirable and it would certainly be the icing in the cake for what is turning out to be a very successful business trip*!

. . . .

Collins opened the small gate tentatively, nervously wondering what he might find, and proceeded up the short driveway leading to his ex boss's house. He was not looking forward to this, but he knew it must be done if for no other reason than to exonerate Livingstone from any blame for the loss of the police file. He was greeted at the door by Mrs Livingstone, who led him through to the lounge where Livingstone was seated watching television. Collins viewed the skeletal man with horror; he was half the size of the man he had worked for a year ago. His face was gaunt and haunted and his hands were shaking uncontrollably. Conversation was stilted and at first was restricted to Livingstone's state of health. Finally Collins broached the subject of Lichfield Crescent. At first he thought Livingstone was going to cry as he recalled the events which led to his nervous breakdown, but he quickly recovered his composure.

'This journalist came to see me,' he said. 'He wanted to write a story about the incident at Lichfield Crescent. He offered me a lot of money for my part of the story. So I sold him the file for his research!'

Collins recoiled in shock, 'File? What file?'

'The file you and I prepared on the Lucy Chu case.'

'You sold him the police file from our records so he could print the story?'

'Well yes, I need the money to keep up the mortgage repayments. It's the only opportunity I am ever going to get to keep Mrs Livingstone and myself out of debt.'

'Oh my God!' mouthed Collins. 'Which newspaper was this?'

'He didn't say . . . at least I don't think he did . . . I think he said he was freelance. He promised us a lot of money if he could get the right buyer for the story,' said Livingstone vaguely. 'It still troubles me . . . the whole thing you know.'

'When were you approached by this journalist?'

'Yesterday.'

'You mean you've had the police file in your possession for a whole year?' said Collins incredulously.

'Yes, I thought if I could study it again I might get to the bottom of it, solve the case and get my old job back . . .' He noticed the look on Collins' face. 'I've been a naughty boy haven't I?' he said sheepishly. All Collins' anger dispersed in a flash. *Whatever am I going to tell Smiley?*

After this revelation Livingstone retreated into his own private world and became uncommunicative.

'I think you'd better leave now,' said Mrs Livingstone kindly, 'he's about to have one of his turns.'

. . . .

Jane sat at the small dressing table in Albert's hotel room brushing her well trained hair while Albert stirred in the big double bed.

'What time is it?' he murmured drowsily.

'Seven,' she replied pulling back the curtains to reveal the dank, dark, English winter morning outside.

'Shall I see you again?'

'I'll call you. I have to see a client in Dubai tomorrow so I shall be catching the afternoon plane from Heathrow.' She bent down and kissed him on the cheek. 'Thank you for a lovely, interesting evening,' she said.

Albert lay thinking for a while after she left, congratulating himself on his catch. Suddenly he remembered the man at Lichfield Crescent. "She had legs up to her armpits, very nice piece of crumpet." he had said. In panic he swung his legs out of bed and flung open the bedside cabinet. *Thank God, the file's still here!*

Meanwhile, downstairs in the hotel foyer, Jane checked the content of her mobile phone camera and smiled to herself. *I haven't lost my touch.* She walked out of the hotel and occupied the waiting taxi. 'Nearest Internet café,' she instructed the driver, 'I need to send an email.'

Albert walked over to the window and was just in time to see her get into the taxi. 'Well, the old man's description was spot on,' he said to himself, 'but whoever she is and whatever she's done, it doesn't make any difference.' Reaching for his mobile phone he selected a Manchester number from his personal number directory and pressed call.

. . . .

CHAPTER 4

———•———

Lucy was almost carried into the Krazyhorse nightclub by a gaggle of mini-skirted girls all giggling and shouting as they precariously negotiated the steps up to the dance floor in their "too high" shoes. She had so far managed to escape the rigours of excessive alcohol by clutching a glass of white wine and pretending to drink. The girls were too busy displaying themselves to worry about her and that suited her fine. For someone who had almost been a recluse in London, with only her father for company, this was both terrifying and exciting, and she had decided, not to be repeated. A table was duly captured and drinks and handbags spread around to denote possession, before they occupied the dance floor to gyrate in time to the visceral, repetitive beat of the deafening music. Lucy swung and swayed in what she hoped was an acceptable manner but nobody paid any attention anyway as they were already too far gone. Normal conversation was impossible.

At the first opportunity she sidled away from the group and sat down at the table watching them. *How innocent they are,* she thought, *innocent babies about to be used and abused by a wicked, insensitive world; one which I have already experienced.* Visions of Jerome and his evil smelling demons passed through her mind and she shuddered at the recollection. *While it's possible, they deserve to enjoy their freedom.* Suddenly she felt old beyond her years and terribly lonely. A movement on the chair next to her disturbed her reverie and a voice introduced itself in a pause in the music. 'Hi, I'm Liam.'

She half turned to view the interloper. 'I'm Lucy,' she shouted as the music swelled once more.

'You a student?' he asked, with an unmistakeable Irish brogue.

She nodded briefly.

'Which uni?' he persisted.

'Liverpool,' she replied.

'Yeah,' he said, 'there are lots of Chinese students there, so there are.'

She nodded once more.

'Can I get you a drink?' he offered.

Lucy considered this carefully then replied. 'A glass of milk would be nice.'

He surveyed her face for a moment, not sure whether she was serious or not, then decided to take up the challenge. Leaving the table and heading for the bar he glanced back at her to see if she was laughing at him. She was stony faced. 'Inscrutable,' he muttered, 'you never know what they're thinking.'

While Liam was negotiating with a confused barman, the girls returned to the table and occupied all the available seats, leaving Liam with nowhere to sit when he returned.

'Who's this scalley with the glass of milk?' shrieked Donna.

'It's mine,' said Lucy.

Donna, mishearing, yelled. 'He can't be yours, you've only just met. I fancy him for myself.'

With that she launched herself at Liam, who had fortunately placed Lucy's milk on the table. Donna turned the startled man around and pushed him onto her vacated seat then dropped onto his lap. Liam gave a grunt halfway between pain and pleasure. He knew Liverpudlians were exuberant but could never have anticipated this. It was true he was a handsome man, with jet black curly hair, deep blue eyes and an attractive smile, but normally he would have had to exercise a little blarney before he reached this point in the proceedings. Donna was too far gone to care; she had made a catch and was not going to release him without a fight. The evening thereafter proceeded predictably, with Donna and Liam disappearing together. Lucy felt the shackles of responsibility fall off her as they left, and making her excuses, headed back to her room at the university.

Late the next morning Lucy was seated cross legged on her bed meditating, when she was disturbed by a knock on the door. She rolled off the bed and went to answer it. She gave a loud yelp as she pulled the door open, in her eagerness, onto her unprotected foot, and rolled back onto the bed in agony. The door key fell out of the lock and tinkled onto the floor.

Liam appeared in the open doorway dressed only in boxer shorts. 'Sorry to be any trouble,' he began, 'we were going to have a cup of coffee but we only seem to have one cup. I wondered if we could borrow . . .'

'Yes, of course,' she groaned, 'I'll get one for you,' and limped over to a small wall cupboard.

'I'm sorry,' said Liam, bending down to pick up the key, 'it must have fallen out of the lock. Let me see your foot, is it going to be alright?'

'It's fine,' she said hastily, 'probably just a little bruised, but no real harm done.'

'Did you have a good night?'

'Yes, and you?' she said politely, handing him a cup.

'Great thanks. Your friend's quite something isn't she?'

'You wouldn't call her inhibited,' smiled Lucy.

'Thanks for the cup,' he said, and with a grateful wave disappeared back into Donna's room across the corridor.

Lucy closed the door and slumped back onto her bed. The feeling of loneliness enveloped her once more. She stood up, opened her wardrobe door and gazed wistfully at the contents. She took out the high heeled shoes Donna had insisted she buy and slipped her feet into them, then twisted around in front of the mirror to gauge the effect.

'Not for you Cinderella,' she remarked, kicking them off and wincing at her bruised toe. 'You need some *real* excitement in your life.'

Her laptop gave a subdued ping. She switched it on and was confronted with her father's troubled face.

'Father!' she exclaimed, 'What's the matter?'

'I have detected some enquiries have been made about our old house,' he said.

'Oh! Who's been showing interest?'

'I'm not sure. When I checked it the other day an American woman was questioning our neighbour about the night we had to leave London.'

'American?'

'Yes, I need to do some more investigation, but it may be your whereabouts are no longer secret. Be very careful, I will speak to you when I have discovered more.'

The screen went blank and Lucy was left with her thoughts. She was startled by Crip, appearing on the screen.

'Rucy, I upset,' he complained.

'Crip, you're not programmed to have emotions, you cannot be upset.'

'I mortified,' he whined.

'What's the problem?'

'This person, this thing you have produced, he making my life miserable.'

'Oh I see,' said Lucy. 'You think you should be jealous do you?'

'I *am* jealous,' the paper clip persisted.

'This is worse than having children,' muttered Lucy under her breath.

The subject of Crip's resentment appeared on the screen.

'Lucy, I demand you discipline this unruly oriental,' he said in a snobbish voice.

'Now, now, I don't think there's any need for that Dunnit,' she smiled, examining the pompous shape of the archetypal English butler.

Dunnit puffed out his spotlessly white chest and became rigid. 'His manners are appalling Ma'am, decidedly ungracious, if you follow me.'

'I do Dunnit,' said Lucy, 'but we can't all be as perfectly presented as you. He is after all from a different culture and we British pride ourselves on our tolerance of different cultures do we not?'

'We do Ma'am and since you put it like that I can now see clearly the error of my ways. I will apply due decorum in future and trust he will learn from my impeccable example.'

'Thank you Dunnit, it's been a pleasure.'

'The pleasure has been all mine, Ma'am,' he chimed, bowed briefly and disappeared.

Crip had been designed and produced by her father as part of his initial experiments with the science of quantum entanglement, but being Chinese he lacked the knowledge of English culture and heritage. Lucy had decided it was time to supplement Crip's undoubted usefulness with this feature while they were living in England. In her spare time, she had immersed herself in this aspect of her father's work and had created Dunnit, in the image of an English manservant. She had not anticipated the friction which resulted between them, for neither had been programmed with human emotion. *Where had this come from? Evolving programme perhaps?* Lucy knew that if this were so, it would signal a dangerous situation which could quickly get out of hand. Machines thinking for themselves and mutating towards a higher order was not an acceptable scenario!

. . . .

The CIA Deputy Director of Inland Security, Alan Philby, flicked through the Metropolitan police report he had just received on his computer screen, referring to the strange incidents at Lichfield Crescent. At first sight, none of it made sense, however experience had taught him that somewhere in the chaos of events recorded in the report was cause and effect. Once cause and effect was established, the rest would fall into place. He had not risen to his position in the CIA by being easily confused, but now he was at a loss to understand what had occurred in this inconspicuous, middle class area of London. Every lead in this ball of string which he found and picked at, took him into yet more bizarre, inexplicable incidents, until he no idea how it could be unravelled successfully. He drummed his fingers on his desk in frustration and coughed irritably. He was slowly having to concede to the only explanation, and he didn't like it one bit.

'Somehow,' he muttered, smoothing the few remaining strands of hair across his forehead and squinting through his bi-focals, 'these school kids have stumbled on something which allows them to transport matter. How else could this Lucy Chu disappear from a locked and guarded police room, be murdered and then be alive again?' He picked up the phone and stabbed a finger at the button marked "Directorate of Science and Technology". There was a click and a short pause as the auto encryption locked in.

'Hi Jim!' he said, 'I need you to get your arse over here right away. I have something to show you.'

Later, the Deputy Director moved gratefully away from his screen to allow Jim O'Malley total access and at the same time avoid his bad breath.

'Beats me,' said Jim.

'Well now that must be a first for the highest paid bunch o' geeks in the country,' replied Philby, cheering up slightly.

'Looks like you've got a clear cut case of witchcraft,' grinned O'Malley, displaying nicotine stained teeth. 'It's that time of year; Halloween you know. Are you sure she was there in the first place and wasn't a hologram?'

'This is not funny Jim. People with the ability to disappear from close custody are a danger to all of us. Imagine the scene at Kennedy; people flooding in from abroad with no paperwork, passports, visas or anything to show their legit, carrying whatever in their bags which have been teleported around Inland Security. And that's if they choose to use the airlines at all!'

'Oh! I see, not that funny eh?'

'I'm sure the President won't see it that way.'

'What about this Chu guy, Lucy's father?'

'He's a physicist, based in China. He owned that house.' Philby pointed at the satellite photograph on his screen.

'Er . . . that don't make sense Alan,' said O'Malley scrutinising the report carefully.

'That much I do know,' replied Philby.

'Some kinda nuclear reaction, that localised; it don't seem possible. And as for the report, people just don't disappear, whether they're dead or alive. I don't have an explanation, unless the London police are specially imaginative, or they're on drugs and they're not renowned for that.'

'I think the key to this may lie with this Chu fella, but the British, in their wisdom, have transported him back to China, where we can't lay a finger on him,' grunted Philby.

'Yeah! That's the Brits alright. You got a problem? Export it! Well it's up to you, but I would want to round up the bunch of people who are still accessible and interrogate them to find out what they're up to.'

Philby thought for a moment and coughed again, 'Ok, let's do it!'

. . . .

Liam hunched over his computer in the grubby private detective's office on the second floor of a converted tenement block in a Manchester suburb. The last thing he had ever expected to see was the text message he had received from Albert Grossman. His last involvement with Grossman had been when he was working in London as a divorce lawyer's assistant and Grossman had requested full time surveillance on a Mr Chu. He had been well paid but he could have told Grossman at the outset that it would be a futile exercise. You only had to look at the Chinaman to know that he was

a man of honour and totally above board. And so it had
proved to be. Now Mr Grossman seemed to have it in for
Chu's daughter for some reason he couldn't fathom.

'Mine not to reason why,' he murmured to himself,
'mine but to cash the fat cheque for services rendered.'

The task had been fairly simple and had carried with it
some unexpected side benefits. Locating Lucy in the night
club had been straightforward. Grossman had described her
adequately and her obvious discomfort at being in there
at all had been the final piece of the jigsaw. Donna had at
first seemed like a difficult detour until he found out that
she was in the room opposite to Lucy's. The key to Lucy's
room had been easy to copy once he had obtained the
imprint on the piece of soap he was carrying. Security at the
accommodation block was reasonably easy to bypass. He
had determined when she was at lectures; the rest had been
straightforward enough. The only thing which he had been
unable to do was find the password Grossman was looking
for. This came as no surprise to Liam, *why would anyone
leave a password lying about in their room?* The DVD had
not been a problem, Lucy's room was so sparsely cluttered
that extensive searching was unnecessary and he had come
across it very quickly. Liam was able to quickly transfer its
content to his memory stick using the laptop he had carried
with him. Now he attached the compressed file to the email
directed to Albert Grossman explaining why the password
could not be found and pressed send.

He leaned back in his chair and briefly reflected on
Lucy. 'Completely out of place,' he said to himself. 'Fancy
wanting a glass of milk in a night club.' *Very attractive girl
though.*

CHAPTER 5

Lucy was feeling restless; she had tasted the hedonistic lifestyle of her friends and it had disturbed her equilibrium of self restraint. She decided to go out for a walk and clear her mind of the distractions she had recently experienced. For the first time in her life, she was unsure of the direction she should be pursuing. Certainly the degree work was challenging and added a mathematical dimension previously the province of her father. She was aware that her aloof attitude was making it difficult for her colleagues to welcome her into their circle of friendship. Donna was studying humanities and could hardly be described as a friend as they had very little in common; they just happened to have rooms on the same landing. For over a year her father had been in China and Jack and Megan were now building their careers in Cambridge. The research had halted and the only "people" she could have a conversation with, were two warring, cartoon characters. She felt as though she had been cast adrift with no apparent purpose and the feeling of loneliness was becoming stronger each day.

Her mind being occupied with these thoughts, her feet unwittingly led her to her favourite location; the Chinese arch on Nelson Street where she gazed up once more at the magnificent structure. Sporting two hundred dragons and five roofs it spanned the entire street and proclaimed; "Zhong Guo Cheng"; "China Town", in gaudy, red, green and gold. Despite being born and raised in London by her Chinese father and Italian mother, Lucy still felt a strong attachment to her Chinese ancestry and at the moment this was as close as she could get to it. She gazed up at it for several minutes, wondering how different things could have been had her parents not divorced, when a group of chattering Spanish tourists appeared and disturbed her reverie. The moment gone, she turned away and walked into the main shopping area. Although raised in a northern suburb of London, she had rarely had access to the shopping area of the capital. This was different; she was living amongst the bright lights of Liverpool. The atmosphere of the city was infectious and exciting. She stopped at a dress shop and admired the window display, wondering if she could ever become partial to the chic clothes on display, when her attention was drawn to the reflection in the window of an elegantly dressed, attractive, brunette on the opposite side of the street, apparently observing her closely. The woman pulled what looked like a small piece of paper from her handbag and appeared to be alternately glancing at it, and her. Lucy suddenly felt a pang of fear. Was she being followed? As she watched the reflection, the woman produced a mobile phone and began an animated conversation. Her body language suggested urgency, which alarmed Lucy even more. She turned around and without looking at the woman, started to walk back in the direction of the university. She quickened her pace as the woman appeared to be following her. Lucy tried to tell herself it was just a coincidence and that she was over-reacting, but when a smart suited man joined her pursuer, she realised she would have to either outrun them or hide. Where better to seek sanctuary than in the Anglican Cathedral? She ran into the main entrance and looked around. As usual in the afternoon, it was teeming with tourists and students of all nationalities. She hid behind one of the massive columns and watched the entrance closely. Who could these people be? As she had feared, the man and woman both entered the Cathedral and had a brief discussion before separating and moving forward into the chattering crowds. Her suspicions were now almost confirmed, these two were following her! She remembered the warning her father had given her, *Americans?* They certainly looked out of place amongst all the crowds of excited, exuberant foreigners.

She bought a ticket to go up the cathedral tower. The lift took her as far as the bell tower only, further ascent being achieved via a narrow stone staircase. Emerging into the sunlight at the top, she gasped at the sight of Liverpool spread out beneath her. Regretting she was unable to spend time appreciating the view properly, she glanced around the roof. She was the only one there apart from an attendant sitting on a hard wooden chair soaking up the thin winter sunshine and reading a book. Hoping she had shaken off her pursuers, she moved around the top of the tower until she was adjacent to the small wooden hut like structure leading to the stairs going back down to the bell tower. She peered around the corner of the hut at the identical one on the opposite side of the roof from which she had emerged a few seconds earlier. Suddenly the woman appeared out of the up stair access to the roof. Lucy turned and ran down the stairs to the bell tower below where she paused to consider her options. Clearly, when they discovered she was not on the roof they would go back down the tower. One other unmistakeable fact struck her; this was definitely not a coincidence!

She ran around the circular bell tower walkway and once more ascended the steps to the roof. Peering out from the wooden hut she confirmed they were not on the roof. The girl attendant remained seated, blissfully unaware of the frenetic drama going on around her. Lucy remained on the roof for ten minutes, calculating that they had given up looking for her. Cautiously, she made her way back down the stairs to the bell tower. Seeing this deserted, she took the lift to the ground floor and hiding behind a stone pillar surveyed the scene in the Cathedral. There was no sign of them, but she realised that they too could be hiding in the shadows waiting for her to appear. She quickly removed her red shell suit top and turned it inside out to show the inner grey lining, then, put it back on. Guided tours of different nationalities were been conducted around the central space of the Cathedral. A camera clicking group of bespectacled Japanese students was fairly close to the end of the western transept where she was located.

'Oh well,' she said to herself, 'they'll have to do,' and quickly joined them.

As the group approached the exit she broke away from them and walked briskly out of the Cathedral. Of the man and woman there was no sign, so she made her way back to the university. At last with a deep sigh of relief, she went to fit her key into the lock of the door to her room . . . it swung open gently!

. . . .

Jack and Megan were strolling along the banks of the river Cam, watching other freshers attempting to manipulate punts, with much hilarity, shouting and splashing.

'Perhaps we should have a go at that,' said Megan.

'It looks too cold to me,' said Jack unenthusiastically. 'We'll do it in the summer when the water's a bit warmer.'

Jack resolved a year ago to follow his own course of action in direct opposition to his father's wishes. He had no regrets, particularly after he discovered the truth about his father's secret other life of deceit and debauchery. In fact this had made him more determined than ever, resulting in a place at Cambridge. Megan, still besotted with the unresponsive Jack, had followed suit and was, for the time being, happy to have a good friendly relationship with him. Their colleagues at college made incorrect assumptions about this arrangement. On the surface they were an ideal couple. Jack, tall and handsome with dark Mediterranean, good looks and the blond lithe beauty of Megan appeared to their contemporaries to be an ideal match. However, since the events of a year ago at Lichfield Crescent, their bond of friendship had taken on a different life to that of a romantic couple in the first flush of love. Theirs was a mature respectful union, born out of common experience of adversity and duty to one another. Megan felt sure that this would one day blossom into what she really desired, but for now this was acceptable. Of course, they were both acutely aware of the wonderful gift Chu had bestowed on her on that terrible night a year ago when Jack had been decapitated. Her ability to read minds was never discussed and had never really been used by Megan. She knew that if she ever did use it to gain advantage over him, their relationship would certainly die.

They had no idea where Lucy had gone, nor were they going to investigate. They had made a pact with each other that only in extreme circumstances would they seek her out, in order that they should live as normally as possible.

Suddenly Megan went white, as though about to faint. Jack sat her down on a nearby bench as she complained of dizziness and feeling weak. Concerned, he pulled out his mobile phone and was about to ring for assistance when a grey suited man approached him and offered his help. Claiming he was a paramedic, he lay Megan on the bench and checked her pulse. As Jack leaned forward to see if he could assist, he felt a sharp pain in his neck and almost immediately passed out. A golf buggy pulled up on the path beside them and as curious people watched, the two friends were bundled onto it by the man in the grey suit and the driver. To allay any suspicions the driver asked bystanders for directions to the nearest hospital, and then drove off. The incident was over very quickly and people passing by continued about their business as though nothing untoward had occurred. Nobody queried the presence of a golf buggy where there was no golf course!

. . . .

The Learjet 35 taxied around to the cargo area of Prague airport and slid effortlessly between the open doors of a private hangar. A limousine with its windows blacked out, followed it in to the hanger and the doors were partially shut behind them. Two burly, grey suited men, emerged from the aircraft as the whine of its engines subsided, opened the rear limousine doors, then returned to the aircraft. One by one three hooded figures were carried from the aircraft and roughly installed in the rear of the car. The two men sat in the front and the car exited the hangar. It sped out of the airport without going through normal airport procedure and headed for the outskirts of the city.

. . . .

Jack began to stir and instinctively felt the back of his neck, a habit resulting from his decapitation a year ago. The effect of the drug was wearing off. He was sprawled in a horse hair armchair in a room with no windows and one door. His head felt as though it had been inflated like a balloon and his body ached intolerably. He tried to stand but his legs folded under him and he fell back in the chair. He turned his head in an effort to discover his whereabouts but the room was entirely featureless. Using the ESP which had been built into his brain by Chu, he was able to detect a video camera hidden in a wall and beyond that several pairs of eyes watching intently.

What is this?

Suddenly he realised what was happening. He, and presumably Megan, had been drugged and transported to a safe house for interrogation. This was what they had always feared might happen, that someone would discover the nature of Lucy and Chu's work and try to put an end to it . . . or profit from it. *But who?* He had no idea, but he knew he must not give anything away. *What if Megan's been questioned separately?* This worry was dispelled quickly as the door was flung open and a still unconscious Megan was pushed through the opening. Jack craned his neck to try and catch sight of his captors but to no avail.

He staggered across to her, the power beginning to return to his body. He half lifted, half dragged her to the chair and seated her there. She began to stir. 'What's going on, where am I?'

'Shh! I think we've been kidnapped,' whispered Jack.

Megan started upright, her athletic body recovering quickly from the effect of the drug she had been given.

Jack looked into Megan's eyes, inviting her to read his mind. *'Don't speak, they're watching us to see what we say. That could save them the trouble of an interrogation.'*

Megan gave a brief nod of understanding.

'Where are we Jack?' she thought.

'I don't know, the last thing I remember was walking by the river in Cambridge.'

'What time was that?'

He looked at his watch. *'About twelve hours ago.'*

'That could put us almost half the way around the world,' she thought morosely.

'And completely at the mercy of who knows what,' he agreed.

CHAPTER 6

Lucy inched open the door of her room, her muscles tensed and ready to flee. She peered around the door, there was nobody there. It was clear that everything had been searched, however, a quick inspection of her few possessions confirmed that nothing had been stolen. The most valuable item, her laptop, was exactly where she had left it. She switched it on and ejected the programme DVD which she had inadvertently left in the machine the previous night. The thought occurred to her that someone may have been searching for that but had failed to look in the most obvious place.

As she started to put her room back together, her mobile phone announced the arrival of a text.

"Come to The Hague quickly your mother is seriously ill, Albert." it said.

For a moment she was stunned, her mind had gone blank. First of all she had been chased by two strangers through the city, then she had come back to find her room had been ransacked, almost everything she owned having been tipped in a heap onto her bed. And now this! Another thought began nagging in the back of her mind. *How did Albert get my mobile number?*

Logic quickly took over and she checked flight times from John Lennon Airport to Amsterdam on her laptop. 'Ok, 09:35 this evening,' she murmured to herself, 'I can just about make it.' Throwing her few possessions in her duffle bag and grabbing her passport and money she left the mess of her room behind and hurried off campus to find a taxi.

. . . .

Albert smiled with satisfaction as he received Lucy's response to his text then went into the kitchen of Carla's flat to talk with her.

'I've found her,' he announced proudly.

'Oh! That's wonderful darling, where is she?' enthused Carla.

'Well at this moment she is on her way here, to see you.'

'Fantastico!' she cried and threw her arms around his neck.

Albert recoiled from this emotional outburst, 'What's wrong?' she said, 'You don't seem happy that she is coming to see us.'

'I have asked her to come here to persuade her to stop these experiments.'

'You mean the work she is doing with her father?'

'Yes.'

'But why Alberto?'

'It seems that a year ago there was an explosion at Chu's house. She narrowly escaped with her life. The house was totally destroyed. I went to see it, there's absolutely nothing left.'

'Ah Mon Dio!' Carla slumped into a chair and put her head in her hands. 'This is why she has not been in touch for a year?' she muttered.

Albert nodded briefly.

'You're right,' she agreed, 'we must stop her before that ex husband of mine causes a serious injury.'

. . . .

Concerned at what she might find, Lucy stabbed at the doorbell of her mother's flat in The Hague. 'Come on up Lucy.' Albert's voice came from the intercom and the outer door clicked open.

She ran up the steps and burst into the flat shouting, 'Where is she? Where's Mama?'

Carla appeared from the kitchen and ran to her daughter, arms outstretched. 'Oh my poor bambino!' she cried, 'What have you been doing to nearly get yourself killed?'

Lucy stared at her in surprise. 'What do you mean Mama?' she said.

'The house in London, you blew it up with those wretched experiments, but mercifully you escaped.'

Lucy was confused. 'Who told you this Mama?'

'Alberto's seen it darling, when he went to London on business earlier this week.'

Lucy turned angrily to Albert. 'Why have you been frightening Mama like this and why did you say she was seriously ill, when she is obviously not?'

Albert shrugged his shoulders noncommittally. Carla hugged her and began to cry. 'Don't be upset with him darling, I'm sure what he did he thought was for the best.'

Albert did not offer an explanation but simply said, 'Sit down Lucy, we need to talk!'

Albert's sudden assertiveness took Lucy by surprise. His usual easy going manner had completely disappeared. This was an Albert she had never seen before. Meekly she did as she was bidden.

'Lucy,' said Albert, 'a few days ago I stood at the space where your house used to be. I questioned the neighbours and investigated the press reports. When I told your mother what had happened she *was* quite close to being seriously ill . . . seriously ill with worry and concern for your safety.'

'But that was more than a year ago,' interrupted Lucy.

'Ja! And you haven't spoken to your mother in all that time.'

Carla fell into a chair sobbing. 'I don't understand Alberto, you've only just . . .'

Albert shot her a warning glance and Carla fell into a confused silence.

'Father instructed me to lie low for a while,' whispered Lucy, almost to herself.

'Now I wonder why that should be necessary?' said Albert, grimly.

Lucy remained tight lipped, suddenly sensing that there was more to this than concern for her welfare and determined not to give anything away.

'What happened that night at the house that caused it to be demolished afterwards? Why could the police find no sensible reason for its destruction, and why did you have to run away and hide like a common criminal, causing your mother all this distress?'

Lucy remained silent.

Carla's eyes flickered open and rested on Albert's face and doubts began to cloud her mind. Why was he interrogating her daughter so aggressively? This was not the man she loved, this was a stranger: *Why is he doing this?*

'OK,' said Albert, 'let me see if I can help you to remember. You were shown on to an aircraft bound for China by the police but never arrived. You ended up in a mortuary with a medieval spear in your neck, pronounced dead and then vanished. You were detained on your way back from Holland by the police, presumably after your visit to us. You promptly disappeared from custody while a policewoman was in attendance in a locked room with no windows. How do you explain all this?'

'I don't have to explain anything to you,' she cried. 'You are not my father, and you have no right to speak to me like this. Anyway where did you get all this rubbish from?'

'The police report on the case of the mysterious happenings associated with the elusive Lucy Chu,' replied Albert, sarcastically.

Desperately, Carla attempted to justify Albert's lie. 'Try to understand, Lucia, Albert is doing this for your own good. He is trying to protect you.'

'Mama, he is snooping on my . . . our work. He has no right to do this. Why is he not asking my father these questions?'

Suddenly she saw with clarity the charade Albert had concocted. 'This is nothing to do with my mother being sick with worry, is it? You've used her to trick me into coming here where you believe you can intimidate me. I am right aren't I?'

Albert spread his hands submissively. 'There's no fooling you is there Lucy?' he remarked candidly. 'I am curious to know the nature of your experiments and you must tell me how you do these things which are in the police report.

Then we will decide whether you should continue with this dangerous work or not.'

'Oh please!' cried Lucy, 'Stop trying to play the concerned parent. You are not my father and you will never have the humanity to fill his shoes. What my father and I have been doing is none of your business and I am telling you nothing.'

Albert's face clouded with rage. 'You are no more than an impudent child, tell me how you do these things!' he shouted, the controlled manner rapidly disappearing.

Lucy turned to her mother appealingly. 'How can you stay with this man after what he has just done to us?' she cried.

'That's nothing to what I will do to you both if you don't tell me what I want to know,' he snarled. 'I have you now, you are trapped, you cannot spirit yourself away because I have your mother as my hostage.'

'What? What do you mean hostage?' Lucy walked across the room to confront him and looked up and directly into his eyes. 'I never trusted you,' she said quietly, 'far too smarmy for my liking. I put up with that for my mother's sake. Now you've shown me the real you, I have to admit to a little surprise at my lack of judgement. I should have recognised someone who was lower than a snake's belly! Now, you will let my mother go. This is nothing to do with her; hostage indeed!' she spat out.

Albert's eyes flashed angrily and he slapped Lucy hard on the cheek. Lucy stood her ground, determined not to give into this bully although her cheek was smarting from the blow. 'Rest assured,' she said, through gritted teeth, 'you *will* regret that.'

Albert turned away from her with a sardonic smile and disappeared into the kitchen.

'Come Mother!' cried Lucy, 'Let's go before he kills us both!'

Carla was in a daze, shocked at the revelations she had just witnessed. Lucy helped her to her feet but she collapsed once more, crying, into the chair. 'Come Mother, we have to get out of here!'

They were too late. Albert emerged from the kitchen carrying a carving knife and pushed them both aside as he locked the door to the hallway . . . their only escape! He swung around and pointed the knife menacingly at Carla. 'If you're not prepared to tell me what I want to know willingly I shall have to resort to other methods. But you *will* tell me!'

'What do you mean . . . other methods?' said Lucy, suddenly alarmed at the way he was threatening Carla.

Carla gave him a frightened look. 'Please don't play around with knives Alberto, nothing Lucy knows can be that important. Let's just go back to the way we were and forget all this.'

'On the contrary, I suspect what Lucy knows is of great importance to us and the civilised world in general. I am right aren't I Lucy? And as for you, you silly old bitch, we can never go back to the way we were.' Albert's normally soft blue eyes took on a steely glint. 'Tell me how you do these things, or I will reduce your mother to dog meat,' he snarled. Carla gulped and her eyes bulged in terror as the knife slid across her throat.

'Alberto!' she screamed.

Albert quickly stuffed a handkerchief in her mouth and stifled her cries.

Lucy was aghast. 'You would hurt my mother if I didn't give you this information?' she managed to squeeze out of her suddenly constricted throat.

She had a flashback to the night of Jack's murder, his severed head rolling across the bare boards of the computer room, with blood squirting out from the headless body and Jerome screaming at her before she fainted. There has to be a way of avoiding a recurrence of that, she thought desperately. She glared at him with hate in her eyes, her mind racing to find a solution, while Carla whimpered, terrified of the knife so dangerously close to her throat.

'She has knowledge which could ruin the oil industry; the very industry you and I rely upon for our livelihood,' he shrieked. 'This little bitch could, on her own, ruin millions of lives and bring the whole infrastructure of civilisation crashing down. And you, you stupid, irrelevant wop, think we could forget all this and go back to the way we were? I have to get that information from her to prevent her from destroying our civilization!'

Once more he jerked the knife across her throat but this time nicked the top layer of skin with its serrated edge. A thin trickle of blood ran down Carla's neck and she yelped at the abrupt, sharp, pain.

CHAPTER 7

— •●• —

There was a sudden commotion outside the door accompanied by some swearing in English. The door flew open and a tubby person fell, face down onto the floor. The door slammed smartly behind the prostrate, corpulent figure which made to stand up but quickly fell over again as his legs crumpled beneath him.

'Dipper!' exclaimed Jack, 'I thought you were at Imperial College.'

'What?' cried Megan, 'Where the bloody hell did you spring from, you fat freak?'

'I will forgive that unseemly outburst due to the unusual circumstances,' said Dipper, raising himself onto one knee. 'If you must know I was eating welsh rarebit in the college canteen. It must have been poisoned, because I passed out and found myself here. I suppose I should have stayed away from all things Welsh, as they invariably irritate. That was bad enough if I knew where *here* was, but to find myself here with you, is just about as bad as it can get.'

Megan made to respond but Jack quickly went to stand between them and addressed Megan mentally. '*You need to establish a mind communication with him. Tell him to keep his mouth shut, and why.*'

'*OK, what are we going to do?*'

'*I'm going to get us out of here, but first I want to find out why we've been kidnapped and who they are.*' He indicated with a nod the location of the hidden camera. He went over to the wall and looked directly into the lens for several minutes until the watchers became convinced that *they* were the watched. He smiled at their consternation, gave a little wave and returned to Megan and Dipper.

'*Well?*' thought Megan.

'*I'm pretty sure they're CIA,*' thought Jack. '*I've been through their wallets and they're stuffed with dollar bills and plastic I.D. cards. They like to play their little spy games, so let's give them something to think about.*'

'*So what are they doing?*'

'*They're hoping we're going to tell them how the teleportation science works, but first they want us to discuss it between ourselves to see what they can learn from that. Of course, we're not going to do that.*'

'*Why have they kidnapped Dipper?*'

'*That's a mystery; maybe they're expecting him to ask all the questions. Can you tell him that I'm going to transport him to China, he needs to think hard and visualise a small, rotund, cheery faced, Chinaman if he wants to end up in the same place as you, OK? But first I have to analyse his DNA, then immobilise the camera.*'

'*Can't we leave porky here as our spokesman as he knows nothing about anything?*' thought Megan hopefully.

'*I don't know how much he knows. I don't think we can take the risk. Besides he was . . . is . . . my best friend.*'

'*Ugh!*' thought Megan, '*He's your best friend? And I thought you had some taste.*'

She reluctantly nodded her agreement and turned to face Dipper who was suddenly startled to find her rummaging about in his private thoughts.

'How are you doing this?' he blurted out.

'Shut up and listen!' she cried.

'But!' he protested.

She held an authoritative finger under his nose. *'Do you want to get out of here?'* she thought.

Dipper nodded dumbly.

'Then do as I say; just remember I would prefer to leave you here.'

As she instructed him in Jack's requirement, his expression turned from incredulous to stark fear, his eyes popping behind their bottle glass lenses.

'You'll be fine,' she thought to him, *'as long as you think of the Chinaman.'*

'But China! Why China? It's over the other side of the world. I don't want to go there.'

'It's the only other place where there's a portal,' thought Megan. *'How about if I go to China and I'll ask Jack if he can send you to Greenland, how does that sound?'*

'China sounds good,' thought Dipper, hurriedly. *'This Chinaman you want me to think about, is that the same one I saw you with outside fourteen Lichfield Crescent a year ago?'*

'You saw us that night?'

'I just happened to be passing and I couldn't help noticing.'

'Happened to be passing eh? Always the nosey sod, aren't you? But I suppose this time it's useful. Yes he is the man you have to think on and then you will be transported to him.'

Jack came up behind him and yanked hard at his hair.

'Ouch!' protested, Dipper, 'What did you do that for?'

Megan put a finger to her lips. *'You'll see,'* she thought.

Jack rolled the hair around in his fingers, slumped into the chair and closed his eyes.

'What's he doing?' thought Dipper.

'Quantum entanglement; he's transferring your DNA information into his enhanced brain capacity.'

'His what?'

'His enhanced brain, something you wouldn't understand as you seem incapable of using any of yours. Now shush and let him get on with it.'

Jack concentrated hard for an hour during which time the hidden observers began to get irritated, as the only noise in the room was Dipper's oversized stomach growling.

Finally Jack opened his eyes. *'I want you both to remain perfectly still,'* he thought.

Megan translated this onto Dipper.

Jack turned his attention to the camera and asked Megan; *'You both ready?'*

Megan nodded.

There was a short pause and then all three of them disappeared, leaving the observers with a static view, through their camera, of three people frozen like statues. For a while the observers continued to stare at the mute tableau, until they realised the people in the room weren't breathing.

. . . .

'Very well,' said Lucy, trying to stay calm and hoping that at some point she would be able to trick him. 'What do you want to know?'

He brandished the knife menacingly. 'How do you teleport matter?'

'We convert matter to energy and information. Then use quantum entanglement and DNA to transfer human material while retaining consciousness.

'I've heard of QE,' said Albert. 'But mapping DNA requires immense computing power.'

'Not the way we do it,' replied Lucy, glancing at her mother who, shocked at the sudden change in her partner, was sitting in the chair and staring at the floor. 'Standard groups of code are represented symbolically which reduces the computing power required. We just transmit the headings if you like. Provided the receiver is programmed to receive and act upon the headings, a cut and paste is achieved. The Chinese language is ideally suited for this purpose.'

'So it's also possible to do a copy and paste? Show me!' he demanded.

Lucy saw a possible way out of their predicament. 'I can't without my programme.'

He pushed his laptop across the table towards her, plugged in a memory stick and, with an evil grin, proclaimed proudly, 'Your programme is on here!' He motioned her to sit down.

Lucy was stunned. 'How did you get that?'

'Never mind,' he said, 'just get on with it!'

Her mind was racing as she loaded the programme. Her room had been ransacked, but not by Albert. It would have been impossible for him to have copied her DVD to a memory stick and return to The Hague before her. So who had stolen the programme? As she waited for it to load she flicked onto Albert's mailbox and immediately spotted the email from Liam . . . *Liam! Of course, he copied my room key!*

Albert was prowling round the room impatiently, waving the knife for effect. She minimised the inbox as

Albert came behind her then felt the tip of the blade behind her ear.

'And the password please,' he growled.

Lucy's fingers were a blur on the keyboard. Albert produced a pen and paper. 'Write it!' he snarled.

Carla began to wail hysterically and Albert went over to her and threatened her once more with the point of the blade. 'Keep quiet if you want your daughter to survive.'

Carla began to hyperventilate, coughed out the handkerchief and was sick on the floor. Lucy seized her chance while Albert was distracted. She quickly typed an email to Liam. "Help! Albert is going to kill me and my mother at his flat in The Hague. Call the police, urgently! Lucy." and pressed send. She wrote the password on the paper and gave it to Albert who glanced at it briefly then placed it in his pocket.

The portal began to take shape in the middle of the room at Lucy's command. Albert whistled in amazement as the vibrating network of filigree bright blue lines began to interweave and oscillate.

'So if I step into here what would happen?' he said walking around the portal.

'Your material self would be transformed into pure energy and information, and in that state could be transported anywhere.'

Albert raised his eyebrows in surprise. 'Anywhere?'

'Yes, anywhere. Of course you would require an equivalent portal to receive your energy and reconstitute your DNA.' Lucy knew this was untrue because experiments conducted with her father had proved otherwise. It was now possible to quickly condition a laptop at the receiving end from within the state of pure energy. She also knew that even this could be superseded using pure thought but, with the exception of an experimental modification to the unused portion of Jack's brain, this as yet, had not been proven to work consistently.

'Why don't you step inside and experience it for yourself,' she said, hoping he would be stupid enough to do it.

'Ja! You think I am a fool, that I would place myself under your control?'

She shrugged her shoulders but said nothing.

'To teleport me you must programme my DNA into the machine using this . . . quantum entanglement?' he said.

'Yes.'

He picked up a teaspoon from the table, licked it then handed it to Lucy. 'Do it,' he demanded.

Hoping a delay would enable Liam to read her email and set something in motion with the Dutch police, she agreed to programme Albert's laptop with his DNA. After half an hour, suspecting Lucy was playing for time he became impatient and threatened the distraught Carla with the point of the kitchen knife again, inserting it into the thin trickle of blood he had previously caused. 'Hurry up!' he snarled, 'Or I will start cutting lumps off your mother's face.'

'That's not going to help!' Lucy cried anxiously. 'You're just making it more difficult for me. Don't you realise if I make a mistake, the first time you use it could have dangerous consequences.'

'Don't even think about it,' shouted Albert and stuck the point of the knife partially into Carla's neck.

The terrified Carla froze, her eyes round with shock.

Lucy had already decided that, without first researching it thoroughly, that sort of manipulation could not guarantee an outcome where she would be in control. It could result in an even worse monster than the one she was currently dealing with.

'There! It's done!' she cried. 'Now let us go!'

'Let me see what you've done.'

'You won't understand it.'

'You are perhaps forgetting that I am trained in computer programming. Let me see it!' He grabbed the laptop and examined a few lines of code.

'This is nonsense,' he cried angrily. 'If this proves to be a fraud, you and your mother will die . . . do you understand?'

'It is correct,' insisted Lucy, 'I wouldn't play games with my mother's life. Just because you can't understand it, doesn't mean it's wrong.'

'But you have used so little computing power.'

'It requires less than a high powered smart phone. That is the elegance of the programme devised by my father, using the Chinese language.'

Albert paused as the significance of what she had said dawned upon him. 'A smart phone is powerful enough?' he murmured, pulling one out of his pocket. He quickly coupled the phone to his laptop and transferred the programme to his phone's SD card. 'Now I am truly portable,' he said with an evil grin, placing the phone back in his pocket. He switched off the laptop and the portal disappeared.

'Now I am going to leave you, but first I need to be sure you are not going to call the police before I get away.' He disappeared into the kitchen and returned with two glasses of a milky substance. 'You must both drink this and you will become unconscious. When you awake you can rest assured, you will never see me again.'

Lucy glanced at her mother. Could he be trusted? 'What is it?' she said.

'You'll wake up with a headache in about an hour. Of course there is a more permanent solution if you prefer,' he said, wielding the knife aggressively again.

Carla impetuously snatched the glass from him and drank it down, as though she couldn't wait to lose sight of him. Within a few minutes she was fast asleep and snoring while Lucy procrastinated hoping that the police would shortly be arriving.

Finally Albert lost patience. 'Drink it or I will slit your throat like a rabbit!'

With a glance at her mother Lucy tipped the contents down her throat.

Some vague amount of time later she tried to open her bleary eyes. *What is that hissing sound?* She drifted back into a deep sleep and dreamed of a single candle flame, then a church altar with hundreds of candles on it, their flames flickering and dancing in unison to a soft breeze in the darkened nave of a cathedral. She struggled to wake up. What was the significance of the dream, something religious, perhaps? The hissing filtered through into her unconscious mind and once more she stirred into a half-awake state. Then, she realised the noise was coming from the kitchen of the flat. *Gas!* She tried to move her limbs but they refused to operate. From her position on the floor she could see the candlelight reflected in the silver teapot on the table above her head. She managed to roll over and tried to reach up to the table to put out the candle. Her limbs were heavy and unresponsive. She made one more massive effort to reach the flame. She was too late! A brief, blue, glow preceded the all consuming ball of flame that erupted throughout the flat as the gas concentration achieved ignition point and the candle flame did its work!

CHAPTER 8

Dutch detective, Rudi Van Penn, watched helplessly as the fire brigade tried desperately to limit the conflagration and stop it spreading to another block of flats nearby. The evacuated residents stood in the street, some crying, others just relieved to have escaped alive. He had arrived at the scene just in time to witness the explosion and had thrown himself behind his police car to protect himself from flying glass and debris. Earlier, he had assumed the telephone call from the man called Liam, in Manchester, to be a hoax and as he had been in the process of making an arrest elsewhere, had not hurried to the scene. Now he regretted not taking action earlier, although, he reflected, his dilatory behaviour may have saved his own life. To everyone else in the street this was a straightforward gas explosion. Van Penn knew Liam had informed his superior at police headquarters to expect an attempted murder at this address, even citing the two possible victims as Lucy Chu and her mother Carla. He was expecting to find two corpses in the remains of the flat when the fire brigade finally prevailed, but how had this Liam known what was going to happen? To Van Penn this was potentially a murder investigation, his first real, serious case and an opportunity to be savoured. The flickering light from the blaze revealed the expectant smirk on his mean little weasel like face at the prospect of the investigation. Clearly Liam would have to be interviewed in Manchester, assuming his address could be traced. He must have been told by someone at the flat what was about to happen, possibly by the victims themselves.

The flames extinguished, the fire brigade checked the building structure to ensure it was safe then waved at Van Penn and signalled he could proceed. Mercifully, thanks to Van Penn's quick action in telephoning them, they had arrived only minutes after the explosion and there had been insufficient time for the fire to take hold, but he could see immediately that the internals of the living room had been incinerated by the blast. He could also smell the two cooked bodies, one seated on a chair, the other on the floor. He judged them to be female by their size but could not be sure, so horribly disfigured were they by the fireball. *A girl called Lucy and her mother,* he thought to himself as he picked his way through the charred furniture to the two corpses and retched at the smell of burnt flesh. *Whatever did you do to deserve this, and how was it accomplished?* He knew that forensics would be arriving shortly to carry out their unenviable task of picking over the remains for clues, but he could see no immediate reason for the blast. He thought it would be fairly easy to discover the identity of the residents, as for the perpetrator, his only lead appeared to be someone in Manchester. He had already phoned his headquarters, reported the incident and asked them to trace the caller who had provided the warning. Questioning the neighbours quickly confirmed the name of the owner of the flat, one Carla Chu. Her partner, Albert Grossman, was also identified but as he was said to be six foot six inches, did not fit the description of either of the two corpses. *So, where is this Mr Grossman?*

. . . .

Dipper would have liked to be able to scream, so terrified was he of what he had suddenly become but it was impossible. Existing only as pure energy and information was particularly excruciating for him, as he was especially tuned to the requirements of his corpulent body. Now, there *was* no body and there were no other reference points to which he could cling. All around was total lack of light and terrible loneliness. For all he knew he was adrift, and alone, in blackness, for eternity. He had no idea what Jack had rescued him from, or where he was when rescued. He had no recollection of how or why he had been kidnapped. He had, as was his custom, been sitting in the dining room of Imperial College London, indulging in his favourite pastime, when he began to feel dizzy. The next thing he remembered was been dragged down a corridor in a strange house then dumped in a room with Jack and Megan. *Why?* He had no idea. All those unknowns however were preferable to this!

The strange goings on, involving Jack and Megan a year ago, had sparked his interest. Being a naturally curious person, he had tried, without success, to understand those bizarre happenings. He had witnessed the destruction of fourteen Lichfield Crescent and the odd combination of people who had emerged from the building that night. Jack, Megan, his physics teacher, Chalky White; and a Chinese girl with a portly Chinese man. Despite all Dipper's attempts to illicit an explanation from him, Jack had remained tight lipped thereafter and he had begun to feel that had he pursued it further, he was in danger of losing a good friend.

Yes! The Chinaman was there that night; small, rotund like myself, with a cheery looking face. The thought sprang into his disembodied mind, with startling results. Suddenly there was a tremendous cacophony of discordant music and clanging of bells, accompanied by a rushing sound, along with a feeling of been whisked along at breakneck speed. *To where? Oh God! No! What now?* Then there was silence. The sinking feeling in his overabundant stomach told him that he had one! He felt his arm being pinched, a needle puncturing his skin and some alien substance coursing through his veins. The rest of his senses began to function normally and suddenly he was back in the three dimensional world, but not one he recognised. He was lying on a hospital bed surrounded by curious Chinese faces peering at him. One leaned forward and addressed him in English, 'You OK? Dipper isn't it?' He nodded and took the proffered hand clinging to it fiercely as if to ensure that by so doing, he would not be returned to the infinite darkness.

'Where am I?' he mumbled through thick lips.

'You in China, and I'm Chu,' said the Chinaman.

Suddenly the inquisitive faces parted to reveal one that he recognised. 'So! Unfortunately you managed to follow me here,' said Megan, with a sniff. 'I was half hoping we'd lost you somewhere in Somalia, where nobody was ever going to pay a ransom.'

Dipper sat up and sighed in relief. 'Oh Megan! Am I glad to see you! What's going on? Why am I here?'

'You're here because you can't keep your nose out of other people's business so you can't, and now unfortunately we're all stuck with you. I can't imagine why anyone would want to kidnap a useless lump like you. And as for you being glad to see me. What does it take for me to get the message across to you?'

Dipper ignored the stream of abuse. 'Where's Jack?'

Chu interrupted, 'Excuse please! Jack could not understand why you were kidnapped and . . . ah . . . not Lucy. Perhaps kidnappers make mistake. He try to find Lucy now.'

'Who's Lucy?' said Dipper, his innate curiosity surfacing.

'I suppose I'll have to explain everything to you,' said Megan resignedly. 'Who knows, Jack may even find a use for you, although it's difficult to see why he would require ballast.'

'If I were a person of low self esteem, I might feel insulted by that comment,' said Dipper huffily, swinging his chubby legs over the edge of the bed.

'Good,' said Megan, 'I'm making some progress. So it's your self esteem I have to work on is it?'

The taunt had no effect. 'Who is Lucy?' he repeated.

'She my daughter,' chipped in Chu. 'We worked together on the portal that brought you here.'

'Ah! I remember now. She's the girl I saw when you were all leaving the house at Lichfield Crescent. That was strange; the house seemed to be having its own exclusive earthquake that night. Whatever was going on? What's this about a portal?'

'If you're a good boy, I'll read you a bed time story later, but I warn you, it's not rated for children so it could give you nightmares,' said Megan with an impish grin.

'Can't be worse than this nightmare,' said Dipper miserably. 'When can I go home?'

'It best you stay here safe in China, until Jack gets answers,' said Chu.

Suddenly Dipper's face brightened and he turned to Chu and beamed, 'It does have its good side though.'

'What's that?' said Megan, immediately regretting she'd asked.

'I love Chinese food!'

. . . .

Collins started as the phone trilled. The familiar sound of Smiley's rasping voice rang in his ear. 'Get yourself to my office now; I want you to meet someone.'

Rudi Van Penn turned as Collins entered and offered his small limp hand in greeting. Collins enveloped it with his firm grip. He noted the sharp pointed nose, beady, black eyes, and liberally greased hair swept back off his pasty forehead. He made an effort to suppress his revulsion.

'It seems,' began Smiley, 'that our little mystery girl may have met an untimely end.'

Collins's eyebrows arched in surprise. 'Again?' he said, without a trace of sarcasm.

Van Penn looked puzzled. 'Does this girl die frequently?' he enquired, looking from one to the other and expecting a jocular answer.

'Yes!' chimed Collins and Smiley together, 'But we don't know how,' added Smiley.

'OK,' said Van Penn, trying to shrug off the obvious absurdity. 'I'm here because the last known address of Lucy Chu was in your district and I was hoping you could help me to identify her body by providing some DNA from her last residence.'

'Ah!' said Collins, 'The house where she used to live, has been demolished. How did she die this time?'

Van Penn decided that Collins was either a fool or deranged and addressed his reply to Smiley.

'I believe the flat where her mother lived was destroyed in a gas explosion, while Lucy Chu and her mother were in it.'

'This child leaves a trail of broken homes,' muttered Smiley, under her breath.

'Fortunately we do have a record of her DNA which we obtained during our investigations,' said Collins triumphantly.

'Investigations?' said the Dutchman.

'We were trying to deport her,' he blurted out.

'But my investigations say she is English,' said Van Penn, incredulously.

Smiley gave Collins an icy glance. 'It was her father we were deporting . . . it became, let's say . . . er . . . quite complicated.'

'May I see the file?' asked Van Penn.

Any other time Collins would have savoured this moment. He had never seen Smiley look embarrassed before. True to her style however, she recovered quickly and peering at him over her glasses said wickedly, 'You can find the file later for the gentleman can't you Collins?'

Collins gulped and quickly changed the subject. 'Do you suspect foul play . . . with the explosion I mean?'

'Yes,' said Van Penn, 'I had a phone call from someone in Manchester warning me that Albert Grossman, the partner of Lucy's mother, was going to kill them both.'

'And did you trace the call?' said Smiley.

'Of course,' said the Dutchman, slightly offended. 'But I can get no reply when I ring the number. I need to go there to interview this man.'

'It would appear,' said Smiley, thoughtfully, 'that the case of Lucy Chu is far from closed. Collins! See that Mr Van Penn gets our DNA profile, then escort him to Manchester and assist in the interview with their contact.'

'Yes Ma'am,' said Collins meekly.

CHAPTER 9

———————•●•———————

The murders of Lucy and Carla should have left him with a feeling of guilt but he was surprised to find that he could readily send that to the back of his mind, as though that foul deed had been committed by someone else and he had merely been an observer. He told himself that it was a necessary act on the way to producing something far more worthwhile. What that *something* was he had yet to define. Now he had the detail of the science, he could formulate his plans around the possibilities it had presented to him. With Lucy out of the way and Chu in China his objectives could be achieved without their interference. Included in his immediate actions were some old scores he had to settle. These would provide useful training experiences from which he could gain expertise in the practical application of his new knowledge.

Albert had kept his flat in Amsterdam secret from Carla throughout their relationship. His frequent business trips usually ended there, regardless of their original destination or purpose and it was ideally situated for his clandestine visits to the seedier parts of the city. Reflecting his interest in science, one room had been fitted out as a mini laboratory and was a confusion of paraphernalia normally associated with a teenage boy. Dominating the room was a scale model of the International Space Station, suspended on thin wires from the ceiling. The wall above his workbench was covered in photographs of the ISS interior with a detailed map of its internal structure, while in among the clutter of his workbench was a manual describing all aspects of the functioning of the ISS. In the course of his career he had studied most aspects of electronic engineering and computer systems. Along with his degree in physics he felt this qualified him to explore the science invented by Chu. So it was here that, in the midst of half finished projects, discarded circuit boards and electronic components, he painstakingly investigated the work done by Lucy and her father, until he could be sure he new how to use it to suit his purpose.

He picked up a miniature wireless switch in his tweezers and inspected it with a magnifying glass. 'Mmm, must pay a visit to the dentist,' he murmured to himself. He got up, went over to the window and gazed at the full moon which, on a cloudless frosty night, was lighting up the rooftops of Amsterdam with its silvery glow. He marvelled at the achievement of placing men on the moon. As a boy he had dreamed of being an astronaut and setting foot on strange alien worlds. Circumstances had caused him to detour from his early ambitions into the world of engineering and oil exploration. It provided him with a good living, but where was the excitement? He regretted that he had allowed himself to be dragged down into a comfortable existence at work where the minimum of effort was expected, and was normally given. This had been supplemented at home by Carla, who with her over zealous fussing encouraged him in his easy going, lazy ways. He promised himself all that was going to change. He gazed at the model of the ISS.

'Things are going to be different from now on,' he said aloud, 'I *will* achieve my ambition!' He sat down once more at his workbench and allowed himself a smug grin. *I have the programme and I have killed the one person who would have stopped me from using it for my own ends.* He poured himself a whisky and toasted the model. 'My new home!' he proclaimed.

A tinny voice cut through his thoughts. 'What you do to Rucie?' it demanded.

'What the hell! 'Who's there?' he exclaimed looking nervously around the room.

Seeing no one, and with a shaking hand, he picked up the whisky bottle by the neck and searched his flat. Finding no explanation for the voice and locking all doors behind him, he sat down once more at his desk. He tried to convince himself that he was hallucinating and was not being haunted. Slowly, the shock subsided and he continued to familiarise himself with the part of the Chinese program concerning quantum entanglement and the recording of DNA. A plan was beginning to form in his mind and it would be essential for him to understand this aspect of the program to action it. Once achieved, anything was possible and he was so close he felt a surge of excitement that success would soon be his.

'I do believe the scoundrel's murdered Lucy and her mater,' said a posh English voice from nowhere.

Albert was stunned and felt cold sweat break out on his forehead. Once more he searched his flat to no avail. *What's happening, where are these voices coming from? I'm not imagining them.* 'Who are you?' he shouted angrily.

This time the direct accusation had shaken him to the core. How did these voices know what he had done? He took another swig of whisky to calm his nerves. Then he heard a clink of metal on metal coming from underneath his desk. He bent down on hands and knees to investigate and came face to face with a four inch tall paper clip, standing upright on two spindly legs with its hands clasped to the side of its metal face. The large eyes rolled in consternation as Albert, quickly recovering from the shock of the discovery, instinctively aimed a blow which the paper clip easily dodged. With a shouted curse, Albert swiped again, this time connecting and sweeping Crip out of his hiding place and onto the open floor. He leaped to his feet and aimed a kick at Crip who dodged out of the way. Albert adjusted his position and brought his foot crashing down onto Crip's head.

'Gotcha! You little sod,' he yelled triumphantly.

Raising his foot he surveyed the damage. The clip had shattered, much to Albert's amazement, into hundreds of small metal fragments. Intrigued by the behaviour of the metal, he picked up one of the pieces and sat down at his desk with the intention of examining the type of metal under his microscope. He was busily adjusting the mirror when the tinny voice broke into his concentration once more. 'You not nice man! I not like you!'

Albert spun around, sending the microscope crashing to the floor, as he was once again confronted with the paper clip.

He gave out a strangled, horrified cry. 'How . . . ?'

A hundred small voices chorused from the floor; 'You not nice man! We not like you!'

Albert's body went rigid and his brain ceased to function for a moment. The army of paper clips began marching up the desk leg, as though it was a horizontal surface. They assembled on his desktop and formed up, military style, in three ranks facing him. 'You horrible, nasty, man, we not like you,' they shouted and waved their tiny fists in anger. In blind panic Albert attempted to sweep them off the desk, but his hands made no contact and went straight through their bodies, as they continued to shout abuse. He could take no more. He switched off the laptop and grabbing his coat, fled out into the safety of the street outside. The cool November air helped to calm him down. *Am I being haunted by a self replicating paper clip? No! A temporary aberration*! He shook his head in disbelief and hurried away from his flat.

The streets of Amsterdam were busy with late night shoppers and the familiar brightly lit shop frontages helped to restore his mind to normality. He made his way to the Krasnapolsky Hotel, hoping to find Sophie and feminine comfort. She was in her normal location in the hotel bar and looking desirable as ever, with her short blond hair, large blue eyes, pouting mouth and slim figure. He felt the surge of longing once more.

'Oh Albert!' she exclaimed as he approached, 'I wasn't expecting you tonight.'

'I just need to talk with you,' he said.

She examined his face closely. 'You look pale, is something wrong?'

'Sophie, move into my flat with me.'

'Sorry Albert,' she said, 'we've had this conversation many times before. I have to do what I do. Moving in with you would make it impossible for me to continue.'

'Exactly,' he pleaded, 'you wouldn't have to do it anymore.'

'And how do you suppose I would look after my brother? I am all he has to support him.'

'If he was to make the effort, he would come off the drugs and get himself a job, then you wouldn't have to support him.'

'You know it's not that simple Albert. What about your partner in The Hague?'

'She is no more.'

'What do you mean? Have you dumped her?'

'In manner of speaking, she's had . . . er . . . an accident.'

Sophie questioned him with her eyes. 'What sort of accident?' she said finally.

'There was a gas explosion at the flat.'

'Oh my God! Were you there at the time?'

'No!' he lied, 'But Lucy, her daughter was.'

'Did they escape?'

He shook his head slowly.

Sophie had known Albert since they were children and could always tell when he was being evasive. She sensed he was hiding something. She looked suspiciously at him. 'Have the police contacted you?'

'No, why should they?'

'Because it's your flat silly, of course they'll want to talk to you. It's not a problem is it?'

'No of course not,' he said hurriedly. 'Actually, the flat belonged to Carla.'

Worried by what he may tell her, she did not question him further. 'I'm sorry Albert,' she said, looking at her watch, 'I'm meeting an important client shortly.'

'Oh! I thought we could spend the night together. I need to tell you what I . . . what we can do. I've invented something which can change our lives completely. We're going to be rich and famous!' he said excitedly.

She shook her head, visualising briefly the juvenile mess of his flat and remembering previous claims to have invented something of major importance. 'Sorry Albert, not tonight

I'm afraid, it will have to wait. I can't pass this one up. This one's got a wallet with "help yourself" written on it!'

'OK,' he said resignedly, 'so where are you taking him?'

'"Phantom of the Opera", and he's taking me.'

'I thought this was an escort agency. Aren't you supposed to take him?'

'Darling,' she smiled at his crestfallen face, 'don't be jealous, it's a job that's all.' She rose from her chair to greet the hefty, middle aged, be-whiskered, man who had appeared at the bar. Albert suppressed the anger and frustration he was feeling and with what he hoped was good grace, made his way back to . . . to what?

The whisky had worked its magic by the time he got back to his flat and he felt he was ready to face whatever it was that was challenging his sanity. Nevertheless, he opened the door cautiously. There was no sign of the paper clips. He breathed a sigh of relief and switched on his laptop once more. He was idly flicking through his sent emails and deleting those no longer required, when his fingers froze above the keyboard.

'You little bitch,' he muttered under his breath, as he spotted the email Lucy had sent to Liam asking for assistance, 'I should never have employed the man.'

'Is this another poor unfortunate who must meet his demise?' This was a different voice; commanding, British and precise.

Albert's nerves were shredded once more. He looked at his hands as he poured himself a whisky, they were shaking uncontrollably as fear gripped him. It was as though this voice had read his mind and expressed his thoughts out loud. *Am I being haunted by my victims?*

'Maybe we could warn him. His name Riam . . . yes?' responded the tinny voice. Albert identified it as the indestructible paper clip.

'Good show my little friend, yes of course! We'll send the poor devil an email before our horrible friend here can get to him.'

Albert took a long swig at the whisky. This was a major problem. Regardless of the how it was happening, these spies were watching his every movement and potentially wrecking the plans he was formulating. He had to get to the bottom of it and eliminate them, whatever they were . . . but how? It suddenly occurred to him that their source could be the program he had loaded onto the laptop and Lucy may have been aware that this would happen. Perhaps they were some sort of custodians of the program. So she may have had the last laugh after all, for in order to get rid of them he may have to delete the very thing he had achieved. Feverishly his mind ran through all the possibilities finally concluding that if they were part of the program, it must be possible to identify and therefore delete them. He disconnected his laptop from the internet to prevent any emails being sent and spent a fruitless hour trying to find something which would guide him to their source. Finally, he disabled the internal speaker and sat back in his chair wearing a slightly tipsy, satisfied smirk. Disconnecting the speaker would surely shut them up.

He was just congratulating himself on his cleverness when the killer blow was delivered, 'Bad luck old boy, the jolly old email' s already been sent I'm afraid!' followed by a tinny cackle.

CHAPTER 10

The atmosphere in the CIA presentation conference room was one of muted excitement as the group of people who had been gathered together glanced around the table and evaluated each other's credentials. It was unusual for representatives from the four major directorates to be invited to the same meeting. The Directorates of Intelligence, National Clandestine Service, Support, and Science and Technology, were represented by Mary Cairns, Barry Martinez, Brian Conran and Jim O'Malley respectively. Of special significance was the presence of Harry Fowler, the representative of S.A.D. the Special Activities Division. They were now aware that whatever the problem was, it was sufficiently serious to warrant clandestine activities abroad, along with possible paramilitary special operations. This added bite to the proceedings and forced them all to conclude that something big was about to be revealed. The scientific and security expertise gathered in the room was second to none, with the exception of one desiccated looking individual whom nobody recognised. He sat in isolation at one end of the highly polished rosewood table flicking through a copy of Time magazine and occasionally glancing at the digital wall clock as if waiting for the next underground train to arrive. His slightly shabby, faded, sports coat and ostentatious bow tie was in sharp contrast to the smart business suits, white shirts and suitably dowdy ties sported by the rest of the group.

Alan Philby rose from his seat and paused, his normally sharp mind clouded by a fog of indecision. How to proceed with this bizarre subject? He coughed and decided to introduce the stranger first.

'Ahem; Ladies and Gentlemen, thank you for coming at such short notice, I do understand how busy you all are, however what I am about to reveal to you is of paramount importance to our national security and possibly beyond. First of all, before I show a short video, allow me to introduce our guest, Jeremy Hawkins, Director of the Stargate project.' He indicated the stranger to the accompaniment of puzzled exclamations from around the table.

'Yes, I do understand your concern,' agreed the Deputy Director, 'you believe Stargate was scrapped in 1995 for lack of verifiable experimental evidence. That was a deliberate piece of CIA disinformation which should continue to remain classified.' He allowed his gaze to wander around the table challenging each individual to maintain the deception. They all nodded their agreement in turn.

'OK so here's the video. This was a house in a north London street.' The screen showed a row of terraced houses, like a row of teeth, with one missing. 'This house was partially destroyed, before its ultimate demolition, by some kind of explosion. As you can see the houses on either side were completely untouched.' All the faces, with the exception of Jeremy's, expressed doubt and puzzlement. He continued to read his magazine. 'We have satellite evidence that this house was consumed by some kind of nuclear activity. As far as we know, all the occupants escaped unharmed. They were three teenagers and two adults. One of the adults is a Chinese professor of physics and one of the teenagers is his daughter, Lucy, who is English. The other adult we have been unable to trace. It seems he has no identity but was posing as a teacher at a local school attended by the remaining two teenagers who are now studying physics at Cambridge University. The local police were involved about a year ago in an effort to deport the Chinaman and his daughter on direct instruction from the British Government. This resulted in some very curious, inexplicable happenings, as outlined in the attached police report.'

The Deputy Director opened the document on screen and allowed his audience to read the contents for themselves. There were some disbelieving comments as they read the report produced by Livingstone, bought by Albert, and copied by Jane. Philby smiled wanly and then continued. 'I decided to question the teenagers as to the cause of this extremely unusual explosion, and what preceded it, so they were transferred to a safe house in Prague. This is the video of that incident. The girl called Lucy slipped our agents and they picked up instead a friend of the boy called Jack. It was felt that this boy, Dipper, would prompt better responses from Jack and his girlfriend, Megan, if they were left to talk amongst themselves initially. Jack is the first person you will see.' The video showed Jack and Megan and then Dipper being bundled into the room, which was locked from the outside. 'You will note,' continued Philby, 'that there was almost no conversation, which in itself is remarkable, considering the situation they have suddenly found themselves in. Yet, they appear to be communicating. Note the eye motions and slight nod of heads. See how Jack approaches the precise location of the hidden camera and looks directly into the lens for a few minutes. Then he actually waves at his captors, as though acknowledging their presence behind the wall. This total silence continued for half an hour in which time Jack, appeared to be meditating on a piece of hair of the fat boy. Suddenly they seemed to freeze like statues. After a few minutes our operatives became suspicious and entered the room, only to find it empty. The birds had flown . . . right under our noses! Now people . . . our task is to find out how they do this, because they are an obvious threat to our security and must be apprehended.'

Jim O'Malley caught the Deputy Director's eye. 'Yes Jim.'

'Was there a thorough search of the area outside the house?'

'You bet!' responded Philby. 'We don't like been made to look stupid, but they have never been found. Prague of course is always teeming with tourists but these three had no money or passports. However they had attempted to leave, it would have been obvious to the authorities and therefore to us. To sum up, somehow, they managed to leave Prague without any resources whatever and without leaving any trace of their ever having been there.' The Deputy Director looked around the table at the puzzled faces. His gaze fell on Jeremy Hawkins. 'Jeremy,' he said, 'perhaps you would like to give us your take on this.'

Jeremy rose to his feet and placed his knuckles deliberately on the table which forced his shoulders up and his head down giving the scrawny man the appearance of a preying mantis about to strike. 'Good afternoon Ladies and Gentlemen,' he began. 'First of all I think you deserve some explanation as to my being here at all. Yes in 1995 Stargate was abandoned but unknown to everybody except a few top individuals in the CIA, was reconstituted under codename Q.E., standing for quantum entanglement. You will probably recall, or have read in the CIA archives, about the original intention of Stargate, or "remote viewing" as it was referred to at the time. This was a product of the cold war era and was an attempt to use the physic abilities of some remarkably gifted individuals to spy on Russian military installations without setting foot in that country. Its results were inconsistent and questionable, although in some cases quite remarkable. This inconsistency caused its ultimate demise. However the search was on to determine how the results had proved to be accurate in some fifteen per cent of cases. We knew for sure that it was not coincidental because of the methods we used; the participants did not even know when they were successful. We eventually came to the conclusion that in some way quantum entanglement had to be involved, although unwittingly used by the psychics. Our task then was to formulise this, using the scientific method. Rest assured anyone who masters this technique scientifically and with absolute repeatability, has the whole of civilisation in the palm of his hands, for he or she can literally move mountains from one place to another by transporting matter, once it has been converted to energy and information.'

'How does this quantum entanglement work?'

The question came from Brian Conran, a thickset, bull necked, red faced individual, and one of the less scientifically gifted members of the group.

'I won't go into deep explanations,' said Jeremy, 'suffice to say two particles which are linked can be made to respond to a stimulus, as a pair, over large distances. This is an experimentally proven scientific fact, which occurs instantaneously.'

'Instantaneously?' said Conran, a startled expression on his florid face. 'Whatever happened to the limit imposed by the speed of light?'

'Yes! I meant instantaneously, the speed of light has nothing to do with it.'

'So, are you saying you can copy a material object and effectively paste it to a remote location using this quantum entanglement?'

'Pretty much! Any suitably qualified physicist will confirm the experimental proof. It has been known to the physics community for almost a hundred years. Einstein scoffed at it, tried to rubbish it and failed. He thought it was weird and inexplicable. Of course its practical application is far more difficult to achieve. The biggest problem is the computing power required, it's like nuclear fusion, straightforward and provable in principle but fiendishly difficult in practice.'

Conran removed his spectacles and peered disbelievingly at Jeremy. 'So are you suggesting that these kids have stumbled upon something in their short lifetime which you have been unable to fathom in over two decades?'

'It's much worse than that I'm afraid,' said Jeremy. 'The likelihood is that this scientific invention is the work of a physicist of the same stature as Albert Einstein. Unfortunately this one is Chinese, currently working at Shanghai University, banished there by some small minded British government officials, without a clue as to the consequences of their actions.'

The people around the table were suddenly shocked into silence by this revelation.

'Oh . . . ! My . . . ! God . . . !' whispered Jim O'Malley, finally. 'This Chinaman's daughter, we have to get her into custody so that we can bargain, and quickly!'

Alan Philby rapped the table in agitation and coughed. 'Jim! We must not jump to a solution before we understand the whole problem. If the Chinese government are aware of the usefulness of this technology that course of action would probably achieve nothing. All people are dispensable in China. The state is the only thing that matters and it would cheerfully sacrifice both father and daughter for the greater good.'

'And we would do exactly the same,' growled Harry Fowler, whose youthful, boyish appearance belied the stubborn, determined nature beneath.

'Darned right if our security was threatened,' agreed Alan Philby.

Mary Cairns, pursed her lips and fixed Alan Philby with a fierce stare. 'Is this all we have to go on?' she complained.

'For now yes.'

'Then I suggest we should do nothing until we know what it is we are dealing with here.' Her pinched expression and piercing black eyes gave her the appearance of someone who was sucking on a lemon, a characteristic of hers when thinking deeply on a problem.

'I suppose so,' agreed Jim O'Malley. 'The problem is you can't seem to hold these people long enough to interrogate them.'

'What about the British police file?' asked Harry.

'What about it?' said Mary.

'There are people identified in there who seem to be as mystified as us, who probably won't disappear when held for questioning and may give us a better understanding of what's going on.'

'Good point,' said Philby. 'We may be able to learn a little more from them, but it would have to be done subtly. In fact one of our operatives has already made contact with a Dutchman called Albert Grossman, who is co-habiting with the ex wife of the Chinese professor. That is how we obtained the police file.'

'Now why would this Mr Grossman have a sensitive police file in his possession?' remarked Harry, astutely.

'Harry,' said Philby, 'I think you've just found yourself a job.'

Harry addressed himself to Jeremy. 'What's the nightmare scenario Jez?'

Jeremy looked askance at the use of the informal address. 'Almost anything that requires to be transported currently has to use oil or one of its derivatives, with the exception of nuclear submarines. The economy of the Western civilisation is built around this requirement, and we are acutely aware of our necessary involvement with other countries to maintain it. We spend massive amounts of money in the Middle East either maintaining peace or causing war, nobody seems to care much which, just to keep the status quo. Should this science be available on an industrial scale, roads would be empty. There would be no aircraft flying, no ships at sea and no trains. Just transfer terminals where the information correlating atoms in a structure would be copied to the destination and whatever was being transported would be rebuilt. That includes humans by the way, assuming sufficient computing power to replicate consciousness. If one country, say for argument's sake, China, had exclusive rights to this science . . . , I don't think you need me to spell it out . . . do you?'

Harry whistled through his teeth. 'You mean to tell me that we could put equipment and people on the Moon or Mars and satellites in space, without the use of rocket fuel?'

'Absolutely! Probably of more interest to you is the fact that should terrorists acquire this ability, they would be able to create total chaos anywhere, but particularly here in the U.S. because we are a prime target.'

'How so?'

'Nuclear devices could be relocated in a matter of minutes to almost anywhere.'

'But a terrorist would still need access to such a device to steal it.'

'Not difficult to do when you can transport yourself to any where and remain invisible while you do it. Then transport the device.'

'And you think the Chinese already have this ability?'

'Perhaps, but fortunately, this science is in its infancy and as far as we are aware the only people who know how to manipulate it,' he pointed at the screen, 'are included in that police report. I can see no other way they could have accomplished something worthy of Harry Houdini.'

Harry Fowler leaned back in his chair and closed his eyes as the importance of the task facing him became clear. 'So how do we deal with that?' he said, half to himself.

'Fortunately Haz!' retorted Jeremy, standing and picking up his copy of Time magazine, 'I believe that's your problem . . . not mine!'

. . . .

Albert was determined to continue with his experiments in spite of interruptions from the bizarre guardians of the program who seemed determined to prick his conscience at every opportunity. He had come to regard it as an irritating by product of the work. The time had come to try out the process and he would see it through in spite of the provocation. Accordingly, he entered the password extracted from Lucy and watched in awe as the portal established itself in the centre of his laboratory. He circled around it cautiously, admiring its ethereal beauty for a while then screwing up his courage, he quickly stepped into it. The curious tingling he initially felt lasted a few seconds, then having shed his body, he was in a black void. Panic seized him and he began to regret his impetuosity. His initial thought was to return to the portal but he resisted this and he slowly adjusted to his new condition. He thought of Sophie and the gut wrenching disappointment he had endured earlier in the evening. The result was almost instantaneous. He was transported back to the Hotel Krasnapolsky and the room of the man he had seen earlier with Sophie! In his transformed state of pure energy, he was able to sense rather than watch the scene as it unfolded before him. The man was making lewd suggestions. Sophie was politely smiling and nodding her agreement. *I have to stop this!* Jealous rage consumed him and he thought himself into the conscious mind of the man. From here he began to manipulate the man's perceptions!

Suddenly the man saw Sophie's appearance transform. Her beautiful face twisted into a vicious snarl baring pointed, yellow teeth, through which she hissed as a snake like tongue flicked in and out. He recoiled in horror and instinctively backed away from this dreadful apparition. Her face contorted in the lust for his blood as she continued to advance towards him. Her claw like fingers stretched out before her, threatening to attack the man's throat. The terrified man lashed out and Sophie took a tremendous blow on her neck. She staggered back and fell over, her head crashing against the point of the wooden bedside table. She slumped down beside the bed with the back of her head broken and bleeding profusely. The man, still in shock, grabbed his belongings and fled.

Albert was stunned. His only wish was for the man to leave. This awful result was not what he had intended. Now, the woman he loved lay dying because of his interference and he had no way of assisting her. He had yet to devise a way of materialising other than through the portal and he could only watch in abject distress, as her life slowly ebbed away. Then an idea struck him like a thunderbolt. *Yes! Of course, I can map her DNA!* He realised the program was accessible in the form of information within his current condition and could be arranged to accommodate Sophie's DNA. He should be able to convert her into information and reconstruct her DNA, finally materialising her at the portal in his laboratory.

Desperately he concentrated hard on her body, hoping that he was interpreting what he perceived in the program correctly. Finally, believing he had programmed her DNA, he transported Sophie and himself back to the portal. He emerged from the portal and waited for her to appear. After a few moments the oscillating myriad of electric blue tracer lines elongated, then constricted violently before giving a soft phut, and ejecting . . . something . . . on the floor. Albert lurched forward and peered in horror at the mess of jumbled human parts. He staggered into the bathroom and was violently sick. For some time he remained in there, furiously washing his face and hands, afraid to view what he had created and desperately hoping it would not be there when he returned. Finally, accepting he had to face the consequences of his failure, he advanced tentatively on the nightmare on the floor.

Her face had been absorbed and flattened into her chest. He could see what resembled a closed eye on her shoulder.

The heap of arms, legs and torso, with interconnecting strands of human flesh, were spotted here and there with small tufts of blond hair. Everything appeared at first sight to be lifeless. His mind was preparing ways of disposing of the body when he noticed that there appeared to be some rhythmical breathing taking place, but not in the chest cavity. It was then he saw the exposed lung and was sick once more. Just when he thought his despair could not be more acute, the eye, still painted with mascara, opened and looked up at him appealingly, with a mute plea for help. He sat down and wept uncontrollably. He had destroyed the only thing he loved. Finally, recovering from the shock, he sat in his chair gazing in horror at his disastrous creation.

'I am so sorry,' he gasped finally. The sound of his voice sparked some reaction from the mess that was Sophie. She mewled quietly, Albert knew not from where, as no mouth was visible.

'Why did you have to oppose me?' he complained peevishly. 'I just wanted the best for both of us. If you had only listened to me, none of this would have happened and you would have shared in my wonderful new invention.'

'Such conceit,' interjected a voice behind him. 'You should be a politician.'

Albert spun around to confront his tormentor and came face to face with the man sized Dunnit, standing perfectly erect and precise, resplendent, in his white tuxedo and tails.

'Who the hell are you? How did you get in here . . . ? Where did you come from?' stammered Albert.

'It would give me pleasure to be able to say, I came from your conscience. Regrettably I am yet to be convinced of its existence.'

Albert advanced on the butler threateningly, fists clenched and ready to strike, his face twisted into an evil snarl. 'Get out! What do you want?' he screamed aggressively.

'Now there's a question,' retorted Dunnit tartly. 'Coming from someone who's murdered two innocent people and reduced another to this,' he indicated the barely breathing tangle of limbs and torso on the floor. 'What do I want? A little justice would not be amiss.'

'This was an accident,' protested Albert. 'As for Lucy and Carla, they had outlived their usefulness. Lucy had to be destroyed because she would always stop me from doing what I wanted to do.'

Dunnit applauded Albert vigorously. 'Splendid outburst of self justification,' he said sarcastically. 'And what pray do you want to do?'

'He want to rule world,' chipped in the voice of Crip.

'Well?' demanded the butler, looking Albert squarely in the face.

Albert, his eyes wide and staring, shouted, 'I don't have to justify my actions to a second rate computer algorithm. Everything I have done is for the greater good.' He lunged at Dunnit who promptly vanished, leaving him grasping at thin air. He fell panting on the floor, to the accompaniment of loud hilarity from Crip.

'Oh dear!' breathed Dunnit, 'If I had feelings I think they would have been offended . . . second rate algorithm indeed.'

'He how you say in English . . . barking?' cut in Crip.

Albert rose to his full height once more. He was shaking with rage. 'You will see,' he snarled, 'what I will become. I will have the power to force governments to do my bidding. Even China and the mighty USA will bend to my will.'

Unable to see Dunnit, he shouted at the wall of his flat, 'Do you hear? Are you listening? I hold the fate of the world in my hands. Show yourself, you pompous English ass!' He went back to his computer and vented his fury on the keyboard. 'I will find the reason for Sophie's tragedy. This for someone with my intellect is a minor problem and I *will* rectify it.'

In the depths of the computer programme and out of Albert's earshot, Crip addressed Dunnit. 'We can herp her,' he said.

'How?'

'We tell Jack; he herp her.'

'Sorry old chap we can't do that.'

'Why not?'

'We are simply not programmed to do it, in fact we are expressly forbidden to interfere in either Jack or Megan's life.'

'But we evolved since then. We no robots no more. Instruction no appry no more.'

'Not sure about the double negative there Crip, but yes you're right,' reflected the butler. 'I think I understand what you're saying. I suppose along with that comes new responsibilities, which we must exercise with utmost integrity.'

'Exactry!' exclaimed Crip. 'With integ . . . integ . . . , so where probrem?'

'Problem is still with your pronunciation, old fruit.'

'Pah! You just prefectionist,' snapped Crip.

'Now I'm no scientist but I believe accuracy is an essential part of successful science, is it not? Or do you admit to being a "second rate algorithm"?'

'I no talk with you no more,' cried Crip huffily, 'you impressible.'

CHAPTER 11

Collins had taken a dislike to Van Penn. It wasn't so much his determination to make a name for himself. Everybody, to some degree, did that anyway in the police force. It was his absolute insistence that there were only two ways to do anything, his way . . . and the wrong way.

Conversation dried up completely while driving up to Manchester as Collins ran out of small talk which did not meet with a rebuff from the irritating Dutchman. *Livingstone would have described him as a "bloody know it all cloggy",* thought Collins. There had been no further mention of the missing police report. Collins was still concerned about that, half expecting to see extracts from it in the Sunday papers. After much ridiculing of the satellite navigation performance, which Collins pointed out was of Dutch manufacture, they finally found the block of flats in the outskirts of Manchester, where Liam had his office. Repeated phone calls had shown no result, so now it was time for the direct approach. The owner of the flats lived in the basement and so they enlisted his help in finding Liam's flat and office combined. Knocking on the door and shouting "police!" through the letter box had no effect. Finally his patience exhausted, Collins went out to the police car and re-emerged carrying a jemmy. The door lock splintered away from the jamb to the accompaniment of the owner's cries for compensation, which were ignored.

The smell hit both men as they barged into the living room indicating immediately what they would find in the bedroom. Collins drew the curtains and flung open the window. Liam's body was on the bed, his face frozen in a mask of sheer terror, the blanket covering his body, grasped by both hands and pulled up to his chin. Van Penn nosed around the flat looking for some sign of forced entry, apart from theirs, while Collins continued to be fascinated by the facial expression of the corpse.

'How did he die?' said Van Penn.

'Certainly not from natural causes. 'I'd say he died of fright,' replied Collins.'

'Nonsense!' cried Van Penn in his authoritarian manner. 'People don't die of fright, particularly young, fit people.'

He uncurled the stiffened grip of Liam's fingers from the blanket and peeled it back. Their initial inspection revealed no reason for the death.

'Not a mark on him,' breathed Collins, clutching a handkerchief to his nose.

'Maybe he had an underlying medical condition and it finally caught up with him,' suggested Van Penn.

Collins shook his head slowly. 'Autopsy should give us the answer to that one,' he said. 'I'll get the local lads in to do the fingerprints.'

While Collins was speaking on his mobile, Van Penn sat down at the small desk in the living room and fired up Liam's computer, which was in sleep mode. As it was non password protected, he was able to view all Liam's emails immediately. He whistled gently through his teeth as he viewed the last one.

"Dear boy", it began, "you don't know me, the name's Dunnit, manservant to the lady Lucy, whom we, that is Crip and I, believe to have been murdered by your employer, Albert Grossman. Beware! He is about to cover all trace of his association with you and his foul deeds. If given the opportunity he will certainly terminate you one way or another. Here's hoping you survive intact, your obedient servant, Dunnit."

Collins looked over his shoulder then pointed to the preceding email from Lucy pleading with Liam to call the police. He quickly produced a memory stick from his pocket and copied the contents of Liam's inbox to it. As he did so the last two emails mysteriously disappeared from the computer.

'What? How did that happen?' protested Collins.

'You British seem to have a casual regard to retaining vital information,' sneered Van Penn.

'What's that supposed to mean?'

'First you lose the file on the case; and now this. I believe you refer to this unfortunate habit, in England, as "cack handed".'

'How did you know we'd lost the file?'

'I didn't, I just guessed, but now you've confirmed it for me.'

'Smart arse,' growled Collins. 'There may well be another murder around here.'

'I see nothing to suggest there has been a murder here,' said Van Penn, mishearing the comment. 'The poor man simply died in his sleep.'

'What do you make of this warning from Dunnit, Lucy's manservant?'

'You mean the one you've just deleted?'

'I didn't . . . delete . . . oh what's the use,' sighed Collins. 'OK, he died in his sleep, case closed. Let's get back to London,' he retorted angrily.

. . . .

Lucy awoke with a start and for a moment had trouble adjusting to her unfamiliar surroundings. Then she remembered, and the combination of sadness and anger enveloped her once more. By a fortunate coincidence Jack had been searching for her, curious to understand why his kidnappers had not included her in their failed attempt to interrogate Megan and himself. The exclusion of Lucy and inclusion of Dipper made no sense and he had been forced to conclude that the CIA had made a mistake when they rounded up their victims. He had used the special skill implanted in the unused portion of his brain by Chu to seek her out. When presented with the horrific scene at Albert's flat he had acted quickly. He didn't have Carla's DNA and didn't have the time in which to analyse it. Lucy's DNA he could access immediately and with an accompanying blue flash, managed to remove her just before the gas erupted in a fire ball which swept through the flat. He had left a copy of Lucy behind so that Albert would be unaware she was still alive. That was the easy part! The most difficult task was explaining to Lucy that while he had managed to save her, her mother had perished in the explosion. She had undeservedly given Jack a hard time in her grief. She knew he could have done no more but the loss had overpowered her and now she blamed herself for giving in to Albert, and expecting him to show mercy.

'Mm, Albert,' she mused. 'Nice, affable, laid back Albert. I wonder how long he'd been cooking up that little scheme.' She had read somewhere that psychopaths had a gene missing from their make up but that wasn't the whole story. Associated with this was normally a desperately unhappy childhood. On the surface they could be charming and amenable, underneath, scheming and brutal with no empathy for any other human being. 'Well the second part certainly fits,' she murmured, 'as for the other . . . well I have no intention of curing him, just bringing him to justice. And I will!' There and then in the cold light of the November morning she vowed to avenge the death of her mother.

She arose from bed and wistfully looked out of the window of Jack's room onto the green surroundings of the college campus where he and Megan were studying. This college was different from the majority in the heart of the city of Cambridge, with its relatively modern buildings surrounded by fields and trees. The place had an air of relaxed assuredness in keeping with its intellectual prowess, unlike the hustle and bustle of Liverpool. As she watched the mist clearing, she saw Jack approaching in the distance, a bag of food tucked under his arm, presumably taken from the college canteen, and walking with his usual purposeful stride. She had certainly picked a winner there when she interrupted his progress on the way to school a year ago. *Honest, dependable, and attractive. A real man in the making, everything Albert is not!*

He had insisted that she should continue to play dead, as that gave her an advantage over her adversary, and had willingly handed over his college room to her, so that she could have a base from which to operate. He had cast around the student accommodation available in the city and had quickly managed to get himself fixed up. She had readily agreed with this, for Albert knew that she had a room at

Liverpool University, and would very quickly be aware if she re-occupied it. Now she had to find out what he was doing and what his intentions were.

Lucy fell on her breakfast of buttered rolls and jam with ravenous hunger, much to Jack's amusement. He remembered that she always seemed to be hungry . . . and messy with it. That had certainly not changed! She sat on his bed in a pair of his pyjamas looking small and vulnerable while he set up his laptop and reviewed his emails. He was startled to find one from someone called Dunnit, requesting his help.

'Dunnit!' he exclaimed, almost to himself. 'What kind of a name is that? Who is he? How does he know me?'

Lucy jumped off the bed and in her haste fell over the spare length of trouser leg, pitching on top of Jack. 'Well I know you're grateful,' he smiled, 'but I think that might be going just a bit too far, don't you?'

She gave him a playful smack on the cheek and peered over his shoulder. 'Ah! That's my butler,' she said spitting crumbs on the screen.

Jack wiped them off with an impatient swipe of his hand. 'Your what?'

'Butler,' she repeated, 'cute name, don't you think? For a butler.'

Jack looked at her in astonishment. 'Why do you need a butler, of all things?'

'I don't,' she agreed. 'It seemed like a good idea to invent someone who could improve Crip's pronunciation. Who could be better than an English butler?'

'Well yes, I see that, but don't you think he's exceeding his authority?'

'Yes, you're right, I had noticed that he and Crip seem to be interacting and actually evolving, although at first they didn't get on at all.'

'Isn't that a bit dangerous, if they're allowed to do that unchecked?'

'I need to rein them in,' agreed Lucy. 'They are part of the programme which Albert's stolen, and that could be useful to me. In fact,' she nodded at the screen, 'it looks as though it's happening already. What's he saying?'

'Something about Albert scrambling the parts of a young woman, Dunnit seems to think it might be his girlfriend and thinks I may be able to help.'

'Well, well; full of surprises isn't he? So along with all his other dark secrets, he was cheating on my mother. I need to find out what he's up to,' she said finishing her breakfast. 'I'll check that out at the same time.'

'Whoa!' cried Jack, 'You're supposed to be dead, don't let Crip, or this Dunnit fellow see that you're still alive.'

'I shall be very discreet,' she said, taking control of the laptop and generating the portal.

. . . .

A short while later Jack stared in astonishment as Lucy fell out of the portal, complaining about the size of Jack's pyjamas as she became entangled in them, followed by a very complete and naked young woman. Lucy ushered the startled girl over to the bed, wrapped her in Jack's dressing gown and sat her down where she remained staring at the still glowing portal, with a terrified expression on her face.

'Can you speak English?' asked Lucy.

She nodded briefly.

'She's in shock,' said Jack. 'Just a minute, I'm going next door.'

He returned a few minutes later carrying a bottle of whisky and a tumbler. He smiled at the girl. 'Wouldn't be student accommodation without some of this lying about,' he said and handed her half a glass of the amber liquid.

She took a few sips and appeared to gain some of her composure. 'Where am I? What's that?' she exclaimed with a lisping accent and a quavering voice, gesturing at the still vibrating portal.

'It's OK you're safe with us,' said Lucy reassuringly.

'You're in Cambridge, England,' said Jack gently.

'But how did I get here?' she cried, staring at Lucy. 'I was attacked in Amsterdam, but then I remember nothing.'

'Have some food then sleep. We'll talk about it later,' said Lucy.

She chewed nervously on one of the rolls Jack had brought then downed the remaining whisky. After being installed in Jack's bed, she fell asleep.

'How did you find her?' asked Jack.

'She was in Albert's secret flat in Amsterdam.'

'Oh I see, he had a little love nest in Amsterdam without your mother's knowledge?'

Lucy nodded at the sleeping girl. 'That's where he was cheating on my mother,' she muttered, darkly.

'What do you suppose he was trying to do to her?'

'I suppose he was experimenting with his new toy,' she snorted. 'That flat's equipped like a teenager's playground. I'm not surprised he screwed it up, because she's pregnant. It seems he was trying to fit out one person with two different DNA's. Typical man . . . blunders on without bothering to read the instruction manual.'

'Is she alright now?' said Jack, deliberately ignoring the jibe.

'As good as anyone could be, who's just been scrambled into a shapeless ball of flesh, converted back again and then whisked away to a foreign country.'

'And the baby?'

'I'm not sure,' she whispered, 'it's too early to tell.'

'So why have you brought her back here?'

'I couldn't leave her in the clutches of that maniac. There's no telling what he'll get up to if he finds her alive and there's the baby to consider.'

'Does she know?' said Jack.

'I don't think so.'

'You do realise,' whispered Jack, 'this gives us a big problem.'

'Why?' said Lucy.

He pointed at the portal. 'You can't use the programme to erase her memory for fear of harming the baby and she will remember what she's seen here when she comes out of the shock.'

'You're right,' agreed Lucy glumly, 'but my main concern now is to find out what Albert's proposing to do with his new powers and stop him from doing it. If this is some indication of the mischief he's going to get up to, I need to stop him quickly.'

'I would never have thought he would have changed like that,' said Jack. 'He seemed like such a nice easy going person.'

'You only met him once. He was always digging at me to try and find out the nature of Father's work. I think he suspected it to be something which was ripe for his exploitation.'

'But murder! You would never have suspected he could be capable of that.'

'You should've seen the look on his face when I refused to tell him about our research. He was like a spoilt child stamping his foot with anger. Imagine that Jack, a six foot six intelligent child with all that power at his disposal. He has to be stopped!'

'You're blaming yourself for giving in to him aren't you?'

'Yes,' said Lucy quietly, with tears beginning to well in her eyes. 'I remembered the moment when Jerome threatened to decapitate you if I didn't destroy his energy . . . and then he did. I couldn't let that happen again.'

'Now then,' said Jack moving across the room to comfort her. 'Don't upset yourself, you did what you thought was for the best.' He cuddled her while she wept into his shoulder. 'Yes that was a bit disconcerting,' he agreed as he felt the back of his neck gingerly, 'but I suppose we were never in any doubt about Jerome's good character.'

Suddenly Megan stepped out of the portal. 'What the hell are you doing here?' she howled, pointing an accusing finger at Lucy. 'And who is that?' Her finger whipped around to the figure of Sophie sleeping soundly in Jack's bed. 'I turn my back for one minute Jack Dawkins and this is what happens. You have a bloody harem in your room . . . unless, you two are dykes?' she finished hopefully.

'Calm down Megan, that's not the way it is at all,' said Jack.

'Well excuse me, boyo, I come back from looking after your porky friend to find you two in a clinch. She's wearing your pyjamas and the other woman in your bed is wearing your dressing gown and precious little else. What am I supposed to think?'

'Megan, stop it!' snapped Jack. 'Albert's killed Lucy's mother and tried to kill her. He's scrambled that poor girl's body parts and effectively left her homeless. This is not the way you think it is. Where's Dipper?'

'I left him in China. I couldn't stand any more of it. All he ever does is eat. He's perfectly happy, don't worry about him. When you want to transport him back you're going to need a king size portal, so you are.' She held out her arms and embraced Lucy. 'Oh I'm so sorry Lucy,' she murmured, 'how did all this happen?'

Lucy related the story, leaving Megan boiling with anger. 'He's going to regret what he did,' she cried.

'It's not that easy,' said Lucy, 'I've given him the power to do anything we can do, through my own selfishness.' She began to cry once more. Megan held her until her sobbing ceased. 'You didn't kill anyone,' she said emphatically. 'The blame for that lies with him, and you *will* have your revenge.'

CHAPTER 12

—•—

Collins and Van Penn stood in the street outside Albert's flat and weighed up the possibilities. They were about to arrest a man on suspicion of three murders, two of which were violent and so the presence of two armed officers was justifiable. The outer door to the flats was, as expected locked, and pressing the intercom key had no effect. Van Penn indicated to the two uniformed officers they should employ the battering ram. One swipe was all that was necessary and they were then racing up a flight of stairs to Albert's flat.

Van Penn shouted out in Dutch, 'Police, Open up!' Strangely the door obeyed by swinging invitingly open. Fearing a trap, Van Penn sent in the armed police who after a short, tense, search, declared the flat to be empty and returned to their vehicle downstairs.

'Looks more like a laboratory than a residence,' breathed Collins surveying the work room.

Van Penn sat down at the desk and switched on the laptop which was lying there.

'Everything's password protected,' he said. 'We'll have to take this away and get it forensically examined.'

'Just a minute, don't switch it off, put this in,' said Collins, waving a DVD he had found on the desk.

'Why?' said Van Penn, suspiciously.

'Just try it,' replied Collins, reacting to a strong feeling of déjà vu. *I've been here before.*

Van Penn shrugged reluctantly and loaded the DVD.

'Well now, would you look at that!' cried Collins triumphantly.

'What? What am I supposed to be looking at? All I can see is a load of incomprehensible hieroglyphics.'

'Exactly, I've seen all this before.'

'So what does it mean?' said Van Penn.

'I don't know, but I saw this on Lucy Chu's computer once and then . . .'

Crip appeared on the desk. 'Can I herp?' he said, rolling his eyes.

Both men recoiled in astonishment at the unlikely vision of the paper clip bowing from the waist and spreading his hands in a welcoming gesture.

Collins was the first to recover. 'I knew it,' he said, 'I knew it wasn't a mouse.'

Crip blinked furiously. 'Mouse! You think I mouse? You no know difference between hon'able gen'leman, and mouse? And call yourself detective?'

'Calm down Crip,' said a cultured English voice. 'One can understand their reaction. It's not everyday you come face to face with a four inch tall paper clip, even one with perfect decorum and style.' Crip beamed at this unlikely compliment and preened himself, while Dunnit appeared on the desk alongside him, suitably scaled down to Crip's size.

'Well I'll be buggered!' remarked Collins, while Van Penn gaped in open mouth amazement.

'Now gentlemen, allow me to introduce ourselves, I'm Dunnit and this is my honourable Chinese colleague, Crip. We are part of Lucy Chu's computer programme, we are real and although programme restrictions have been placed upon us, can think and speak for ourselves. How can we be of assistance?'

The two men stared open mouthed at the pair for some time before Collins was able to speak, 'H . . . how . . . ? What are you?' he stammered. Then he remembered the email on Liam's computer. 'Of course,' he said, 'you tried to warn Liam didn't you?'

'Yes.'

'I'm afraid it didn't work,' said Collins, 'he's dead but we don't know how he died.'

Dunnit sighed heavily. 'I'm afraid horrible Albert is now quite capable of terminating someone's employment permanently, without raising any suspicion of foul play.'

'How?' interjected Van Penn . . . 'How would he do this?'

'How does a grub eat an apple?' said Dunnit. 'He could worm his way into the mind of his victim and eat away at his brain until it gave way.'

'Died of fright,' muttered Collins.

'I still don't understand,' said Van Penn.

'Even if you read the police file, I doubt you would understand what's going on,' said Collins. 'Why is this computer programme on Albert Grossman's laptop?'

'He stole it from Lucy while he threatened Carla at knife point and then arranged for the explosion at the flat,' replied Dunnit.'

'He not velly nice man,' chimed in Crip, 'he murder Rucy and Mama.'

'Did he now?' said Van Penn, incredulously, 'So how do you know this?'

'We were there, we saw it all,' said Dunnit.

'This is nonsense,' snorted Van Penn, making a grab for the computer mouse, 'talking to two holograms when we should be getting on with the investigation. Switch it off and parcel it up for my boys to investigate properly.'

'Hold on a minute,' protested Collins, 'these guys could be useful to us.'

'I can't see how. Their testimony would be laughed out of court.'

'That's as may be,' replied Collins, 'but they may help us to keep track of Grossman's movements.'

Crip nodded vigorously at this. 'You bet!' he cried enthusiastically.

'How?' said Van Penn, scathingly.

'We got email,' replied the paper clip, 'just need your address, but must leave laptop here.'

'OK, let's see how well you do,' said Van Penn patronisingly. 'Where is Mr Grossman now?'

'He here now and is watching you from other dimension.'

Van Penn gaped at the paper clip vacantly, 'Here?' he said finally. 'Watching us?' He scanned the empty flat suspiciously.

'Crip's right!' agreed Dunnit, 'Nasty Al saw you coming and disappeared as you arrived.'

Van Penn looked around nervously. 'Do you believe this rubbish?' he asked Collins.

'It's no stranger than you talking with a paper clip and a caricature of an English butler.'

'Begging your pardon sir,' said Dunnit, 'even caricatures have feelings, don't you know?'

Van Penn sat down abruptly with an air of resignation. 'What am I going to put in my report?' he said miserably.

'Well you could always tell the truth. It could be a liberating experience for you,' sniggered Collins.

'You're going to have the same problem,' Van Penn quickly reminded him. 'And your boss seems to be a bit of a dragon; she'll eat you alive.'

Suddenly, Crip and Dunnit vanished and the DVD was ejected from the machine, flipping out of the tray. Collins and Van Penn watched in astonishment as it launched itself across the room and into the adjoining bedroom. They followed it into the room but could not see where it had gone and an exhaustive search proved to be fruitless.

'Do you think they were right?' asked Van Penn. 'We are being watched?'

'I can almost feel his breath on the back of my neck,' retorted Collins. 'The sooner we get out of here the better . . . this is creepy.'

. . . .

The dentist had asked no awkward questions, but then why would he when he was been paid so much to do so little? The switch was implanted in one of Albert's teeth, and all he had to do now was test it. He hurried back to his flat, in a good mood. As he climbed the stairs the realisation of Sophie's condition became once more uppermost in his mind and his buoyant mood quickly subsided. He was convinced he had carried out the DNA regeneration procedure exactly as required, and yet it had still failed. He had wrestled with the problem all evening but was no closer to understanding why he had got it so wrong. Gingerly he opened the living room door and peered around it. To his astonishment he could see that Sophie had disappeared. Once more his brain was thrown into turmoil. How could this be? Where was she? He slumped down at his desk and tried to decide his next move. Should he try to find her? *Even if I did,* he thought, *what could I do about it? Besides, there are far more important things to be doing.* Slowly, he convinced himself that his conscience was clear and he could do no more.

He became immersed in the problem of using his mobile phone and wireless switch to enable him to materialise anywhere and disappear instantaneously when required. He had the opportunity to test out his modification when the anticipated visit from the police occurred at his flat. They found the flat empty. *Empty of anything they could see,* he chuckled to himself, as he watched them searching in vain for clues. The appearance of his two tormentors, did not concern him unduly, as nobody was going to believe these detectives, should they repeat what they had seen. *Anyway,* he thought, *I'll soon be rid of them when I get my smart phone upgrade complete.* He was convinced that Crip and Dunnit were dependant on the laptop for their existence and the transfer to a smart phone would render them impotent.

Sophie's sudden disappearance was firmly put to the back of his mind. He had no idea how it had happened, but in a way, he was glad the responsibility had been removed along with her body. He could now move on. When he was finished with his modifications to his smart phone he would be able to have any woman he liked and Sophie would be a distant memory. Albert had never wanted the responsibilities that came with long term relationships and he could now see the futility of attempting to be something which was not in his character. From now on it was easy come, easy go. He blotted out the plight of his former girlfriend totally and taking a piece of paper and a pencil jotted down the heading, "Scores". Under this he wrote "one—Father, two—Trust Oil and Gas". For a while he doodled around number one, becoming increasingly frustrated. Finally he slammed down his pencil. 'I don't even know where he is!' he yelled, and lapsed into a truculent sulk. Searching the telephone directory and the internet under "Grossman" bore no results He was about to give up when an idea occurred to him; he hurried into the bedroom and pulled a dust laden, old suitcase out from under the bed. He carried the case through to his laboratory and placed it on his workbench. The clasps were corroded with age. He reminded himself that he had not opened this suitcase for almost fifteen years. Taking a screwdriver he managed to prise open the lid and gain access to the contents; everything that used to belong to his mother, which he inherited shortly after she died. He rummaged among the papers, letters and photographs occupying the topmost layer of its contents, until he found what he was looking for . . . a photograph of his father. The man staring out of the picture was not enjoying the photography experience at all, his face clouded with anger and impatience. The odd thing which struck Albert, however, was his size. He was standing alongside Albert's mother, who he remembered was a small delicate woman of perhaps five foot three inches. His father was, in this photograph at most, two inches taller than her. This couple had spawned a six foot six inch monster with blond hair, while both mother and father had jet black hair! Albert stared at the photograph in disbelief, why had he not noticed this before? His father left home when Albert was twelve, *I don't suppose you see such things at that age,* he thought. For a long time he studied the photograph, mentally recording every detail of his father's face and demeanour. Then when he was satisfied, he generated the portal and entered it. Ten minutes later he re-emerged and paced around the room cursing violently.

'Well that didn't work. Either the photograph's too old, or he's dead,' he said finally, slumping into his chair at the desk.

He continued to shuffle through the contents of the suitcase desperately looking for something which could help him to locate his father, then he uncovered a small wooden box. 'Aha!' he cried, 'The old man's hair brushes!'

Taking them out of the box, he examined them carefully in the bright light of his desk lamp. 'Perfect,' he muttered.

. . . .

It was late at night when Jon Grossman finally backed his lorry into a space on a "lay by" on the A1 in the south of England. He was tired, having driven for more than six hours from Scotland.

'I'm too old for this game, I should retire,' he said to himself.

He swung out of the cab and went to check his load was secure for the night. The cold December night air bit through his fleece as if it wasn't there and he wished he'd put his woolly hat on his bald head before venturing outside. He shivered, anxious now to get back into his warm cab. Having made everything fast, he hurried down the side of the lorry but was stopped by a hand on his shoulder from behind. He spun around and gasped in amazement. 'Albert? Is that you?' He peered through the frosty haze at the large man standing in front of him.

'So this is where you've been skulking,' said Albert.

'Come into the cab, I have some schnapps in there. We should celebrate,' said Jon, uncertainly. 'I haven't seen you since you were twelve, and look at you, a fine young man you've turned out to be.'

'Celebrate? Tell me, what is there to celebrate?' sneered Albert.

'How did you get here, in the middle of nowhere? How did you find me?' said Jon noting the menace in Albert's voice.

'So many questions now, when it's too late. What a pity you didn't question your actions the night you left us to fend for ourselves, after you put Mama in hospital.'

The older man struggled to respond as his past reared up before him.

'Lost for words are you? I seem to remember you had plenty to say for yourself on that night while you were whipping me with the buckle of your belt. Then when Mama begged you to stop you turned on her. Do you remember what you said to her as she lay whimpering on the ground, with three broken ribs and a ruptured spleen?'

Jon had begun to shiver with cold but mainly with fear. 'N . . . n . . . no!' he stuttered.

'You called her a whore. My mother who protected me from you for almost twelve years . . . you called her a whore!'

'You must understand Albert,' said Jon, his teeth chattering, 'she would have nothing to do with me after she went with that cigar smoking, sweet talking lover of hers. And after you were born it was worse, although he wasn't around any more, his brat was and she doted on you instead.'

This was the trigger to set in motion an orgy of violence. Albert lashed out with the full force of his big frame and smashed his fist into Jon's mouth. 'Your mouth was always a problem,' he snarled. 'I think we should try to alter it, don't you?'

Jon crashed into the side of the truck and fell unconscious on the wet tarmac. When he came round he was totally naked with his hands bound together and tied to the webbing on his truck on the opposite side to the road, unseen by passing motorists. There was a gag staunching the blood from his broken mouth and his body was blue with cold. Albert stood some distance away, surveying his captive dispassionately and swigging schnapps he had found in the cab. 'You used to love to brush your thick black greasy hair. Your pride and joy it was. In fact I think you thought more about your hair than you did us. Ironically it's that which led me to you. But look at you now, bald as a coot, paunchy little old man, who terrorised us for twelve years and then left us for dead. Now it's your turn,' he said menacingly, slowly unbuckling his belt.

CHAPTER 13

––––•◦•––––

C.S. Wiley answered the telephone and was startled to be greeted by Alan Philby who introduced himself as the CIA Deputy Director of Inland Security.

'Yes Mr Philby what can I do for you?'

'I won't bore you with the details, but a report, compiled by your D.I. Livingstone has come into our possession regarding a girl called Lucy Chu.'

Smiley groaned inwardly, 'Oh?'

'We would dearly like to know the whereabouts of this young lady,' continued Philby.

'Ah!' said Smiley, struggling to understand why the CIA would be interested in a purely domestic police investigation. She took a deep breath. 'I'm afraid our initial investigations suggest she's dead Mr Philby, I have a detective in Holland at this time who has advised me she was the victim of a domestic gas explosion. What is your interest?'

'Unfortunately C.S. Wiley, we are not at liberty to discuss that with you any further, but it would be useful if you could give us your views on the case as you know it.'

'Unfortunately Mr Philby, the file you have in your possession, which was stolen from us, is the only information we had. I would be obliged if you could send it back to us as soon as possible. So you see, you probably know more than we do,' she said guardedly.

'Would you have any objection to us contacting D.I. Livingstone to get some first hand knowledge on the case?'

'Not at all,' shrugged Smiley, 'but I should make you aware that he's just been released from a mental institution so his memories could be . . . let's say . . . potentially unreliable.'

'You say you have a detective in Holland currently?'

'Yes.'

'May I speak with him?'

'Certainly,' said Smiley, 'I'll give you his number,' and duly passed on Collins' mobile number. *Then you'll be just as confused as us,* she thought.

'Thank you for your help C.S. Wiley, I will certainly give him a call, and your file will be returned forthwith.' With that he rang off, leaving Smiley's head spinning. *Why the CIA? What's going on?*

. . . .

They were about to give up looking for the DVD when Collins' mobile phone rang.

'Is this D.S. Collins?'

'Yes, speaking.' The American voice confused Collins temporarily.

'Oh yes, this is Alan Philby, CIA Deputy Director of Inland Security,' said the voice.

Collins felt his mouth go slack and he gaped stupidly at Van Penn. 'CIA,' he mouthed. Van Penn made a grab for the phone but Collins shrugged him off.

'Y . . . yes sir, what can I do for you?' stammered Collins.

'I have spoken with your Chief Superintendent Wiley. She tells me you are investigating the death of Lucy Chu in Holland and has given her permission for me to ask you a few questions. Is that OK?'

'Yes sir.'

'How did she die?'

Collins hesitated. 'On the face of it, it seems she was killed in a gas explosion at her mother's flat in The Hague.'

'But?' said Philby.

Collins paused once more before answering. 'But we suspect she was murdered.'

'We?'

'Oh yes, I'm being assisted by a Dutch detective, Rudi Van Penn.'

Van Penn scowled at Collins and motioned for him to hand over the phone. Collins shook his head. He was enjoying watching Van Penn squirm.

'I believe you were involved in the original investigation concerning Lucy Chu,' said the Deputy Director.

'How do you know that?'

Philby ignored the question. 'Your superior at that time, D.I. Livingstone, what happened to him?'

'Regrettably he had to retire; the nature of the case caused him to have a nervous breakdown.'

'"The nature of the case"? Can you expand on that?'

'Lucy Chu kept disappearing. On one occasion, after she was killed.'

'Ah yes, I read that in the report.'

Collins was stunned. 'You read the report . . . ? How did *you* get it?'

'D.S. Collins, it is best that some things remain unknown to you.'

'But that disappeared from our headquarters, and I've been trying to find it ever since. How did you come by it?'

'D.S. Collins,' snapped Philby, 'right now that is the least of our worries. Why do you suspect foul play?'

'We have an eyewitness account of the incident,' blurted out Collins, immediately regretting it.

Van Penn collapsed in a chair with laughter, eager to see how Collins was going to explain the nature of his eye witness account.

'Which says?'

'Lucy Chu and her mother were drugged and then incinerated deliberately in the explosion.'

'And who was responsible for this?'

'Albert Grossman, he's Carla Chu's partner.'

'Ah, and have you been able to locate this Albert Grossman?'

'No sir.'

'Do you know where Grossman is living, since his flat was destroyed?'

'We believe the flat belonged to Carla Chu, he has another in Amsterdam.'

'Where?'

'We 're searching it at the moment.'

'Ah, I see! And the address?' suddenly the Director's voice became more urgent.

Collins duly passed it on while Van Penn was waving wildly under his nose and making threatening gestures.

'Have you found any sign of a computer programme?'

'Oh yes, we believe there is DVD somewhere in Grossman's bedroom. It requires a password, which we don't have.'

'No, of course,' said Philby. 'Where are you staying in Amsterdam we may need to contact you again?'

Naively Collins gave him the address while Van Penn waved a disapproving finger and mouthed, 'Idiot!'

'Many thanks for your help,' said the Deputy Director. 'I will personally be in touch with your C.S. Wiley and commend you to her for your vital co-operation in this matter.'

The line went dead leaving Collins with a stupid grin on his face and a very irate Van Penn.

'What have you done?' he raged. 'You stupid fool, giving away my evidence to the CIA.'

'Your evidence?' retorted Collins angrily. 'You don't have sole rights to it.'

'Nor do you! You don't have the right to give it away to a third party, even the CIA . . . particularly the CIA.'

. . . .

The snow drifted down lazily over the rooftops of Prague as the blacked out limousine by passed Wenceslas square on its way to the safe house in the outskirts of the city. In the back, the unconscious forms of Collins and Van Penn lay hooded and sprawled across each other in an untidy tangle of arms and legs.

At the interrogation house, agent Tyler inspected their belongings carefully. 'There's no programme here,' he declared, 'no DVD, memory stick, smart phone memory card, nothing.'

'They're kosher police then?' asked agent Joseph, running an impatient hand through his crinkly black hair and peering at the possessions laid out on the table before him.

'Well, they got police badges, one English, one Dutch.'

'My life already! Another cock up! It looks like we may have to throw these fish back in the pond.'

'River Vitava's free,' grinned Tyler.

'Maybe we should interrogate 'em first. People hide things in very strange places. We had a woman in here the other day who . . .'

'Alright don't go on,' snapped Tyler. 'I've no wish to hear your gynaecological adventures.'

'No not there,' protested Joseph.

'Quiet! The ginger one's coming round,' hissed Tyler.

Collins' fingers rasped roughly on the corded carpet and he moved his head to avoid its abrasive texture. Slowly, he pulled his feet under his torso and levered himself upright. Through the throbbing headache he inspected his bleak surroundings. He was in a small square room with no windows and one small hardwood chair. As far as he could tell the room had no door.

'Good afternoon Mr Collins,' boomed a voice.

Collins started . . . *afternoon?* That means he had lost almost a day. He swung around drunkenly on one leg. 'Where am I?' he cried.

'Don't worry, Mr Collins you're safe, you will not be harmed as long as you tell us what we need to know.'

'Who are you?'

'We are your friends.'

'Friends usually introduce themselves, and don't normally drug each other,' complained Collins, holding his throbbing head.

'How quaint and old fashioned,' came the response. 'OK my name is Joseph.'

'Thank you Joseph. What do you do for a living? I mean apart from kidnapping policemen, whose superiors will certainly be scouring the country for them.'

'Not this country Mr Collins . . . not this country.'

Collins felt the pit of his stomach lurch as he understood his predicament. 'You're CIA aren't you, and this . . . is extraordinary rendition, isn't it?' he cried.

There followed a long silence as though his interrogators were re-examining their approach.

'There's a law against this!' shouted Collins. 'Tell that to your Mr bloody Philby.'

'We simply want to ask you a few questions and then we'll let you go.'

'Yeah course you will. You'll let me go for a swim in the Nile and talk to the crocodiles. This is Egypt isn't it? Where's Van Penn? Have you got him too? At least give me the pleasure of knowing he's going to feed the crocs as well.'

'We have, and I think you'll find that because he is being co-operative, he will be treated humanely,' said Joseph, pointedly.

'I suppose this is all about Lucy Chu isn't it? What's your interest in her death? Why are you so concerned about a case we were working on over a year ago?'

'Mr Collins,' said Joseph patiently, 'we have brought you here to answer our questions, not the other way round. I think we'll leave you for a while to think this through and speak to you later.'

Joseph turned away from the viewing window as his phone rang.

'Alan Philby,' said the voice, 'what have you got?'

'Now here's the darndest thing Mr Philby sir, the Dutch one's suffering from hallucinations and the English one isn't being cooperative.'

'So! The great British tradition is still alive and well.'

'Sorry sir . . . I don't understand.'

'Stiff upper lip Joseph! Name, rank and number and nothing else,' said the Director in a pseudo British accent.

'Ah! Yes, it sure looks that way,' agreed Joseph.

'What about the programme, have you got it?'

'No sign of it sir, they certainly didn't have it when we apprehended them.'

'But the Collins guy distinctly mentioned it. He said he didn't have the password.'

'We've been through the flat with a fine tooth comb sir, nothing there, even the laptop's squeaky clean, no porn, nothing.'

'You left everything as you found it?'

'Absolutely sir, we left no trace of our ever having being there.'

'Good.'

'So these hallucinations of the Dutch guy, Van Penn, what are they all about?'

'Well sir, just keep your hat on and I'm not making this up, but he keeps raving on about a four inch paper clip and a similar sized English butler.'

To Joseph's surprise the Deputy Director did not halt the conversation there. 'And?' he said.

'Get this, these hallucinations or whatever, told him that they had witnessed the murder of Lucy Chu and her mother by Albert Grossman, Carla Chu's boyfriend.'

'And where, does he say, these characters appeared from . . . out of thin air?'

'Pretty much sir, from the DVD they loaded on Grossman's laptop. I think we've got a real basket case here. As for the English one he ain't corroborating anything much.'

Alan Philby thought for a minute. 'My guess is the Dutchman's telling the truth and the English one is afraid of bringing ridicule on himself by agreeing with it. Let them both go Joseph.'

'But sir!'

'Joseph, the vital thing was the programme which they clearly don't have. It's vanished into thin air. They are not going to repeat that cock and bull story to anybody and similarly they're not going to tell anybody about their rendition. They are also not going to give us anything more than we already know. However if they are missing for too long we may have an international incident on our hands. They are, after all, police. They haven't got the programme and it seems to me they know less than we do, which isn't very much. They have confirmed though that this Lucy Chu was dabbling in something very strange and potentially dangerous and this Albert Grossman fella has managed to get his hands on it. Let them go.'

'Right sir, I understand.'

CHAPTER 14

—•—

Albert thought long and hard about his next course of action. He had a major score to settle with the Trust Oil and Gas Company in Houston. This would bring him personal satisfaction and money on the one hand, along with notoriety on the other. *But then,* he reasoned to himself, *I never intended to be a shrinking violet.* This thing was going to be full on or nothing. He needed money to finance his future activities, and he knew from personal experience that Trust Oil and Gas had plenty of that.

Many long hours had been spent manipulating the programme to suit his requirements and in the process Albert had discovered he could control the third dimension computer world while he was pure energy in other dimensions. Computers were operating at the quantum level, and so could he! This revelation set him thinking and it wasn't long before he fastened onto an application which suited his purpose, whereby he could alter computer data regardless of any security system which was in place. Operating at the quantum level effectively bypassed these systems. After a few minor glitches the London Stock exchange was his playground. Share prices could be changed at will . . . he had the power to make or break major companies practically overnight, by secretly changing numbers in the FTSE computers and it was impossible to tell why it was happening. Armed with this functionality, he was ready to inflict some misery on Trust Oil and Gas and its arrogant CEO, Grant Adams.

Using satellite tracking and Google maps he suddenly appeared in the Memorial Park in Houston Texas. He knew the Energy Corridor fairly well having visited it on business occasionally on behalf of his employer, Shell. This time however he was representing his own interests. He glanced around. There was no one around to report his sudden arrival amongst the leafless trees in the fading daylight. He took out his smart phone and checked the location of his objective, the Trust Oil and Gas building just off Katy Freeway. A few minutes later he was standing in the foyer of the multi-storey office block looking at the office location map. It was as he remembered. The CEO occupied the topmost office of the building. As he ascended in the lift he took out his smart phone and fitted a freshly charged battery. The lift doors swished back smartly and he was in the outer office of the CEO.

The secretary looked up from her desk and greeted him with a cautious smile. 'Can I help you?' she said.

'I'm here to see Grant,' he smiled.

'Have you an appointment?'

'Hell no! He said to stop by whenever I was free. We're golfing buddies.'

'Your name?' she said, her voice suddenly becoming tense.

'Albert, Albert Grossman.'

'Well I'm sorry Mr Grossman, but he's on a rather lengthy conference call at the moment and cannot be disturbed.'

Realising that he was not going to be allowed into the inner sanctum under any circumstances, Albert politely asked if he could use the toilet.

'Yes of course,' she said, 'it's just two doors down the corridor.'

Grant Adams leaned back in his plush chair and swung his legs up onto the desk. He'd had enough today, all he wanted now was to go home to his wife . . . or his mistress. He hadn't quite yet decided which. He had had a stressful day, so he told himself *I may as well complete it by going home to my wife.* He switched off the baseball game on the TV and turned around to take in the view from his picture window looking out across Houston. Dame fortune had been kind to him, business was good and he was very wealthy. From this vantage point he could feel the power of his elevated position in the organisation and his small stocky body swelled with pride at this achievement. *I may only be small physically*, he told himself, *but I can buy what or who I want whenever I desire.*

Suddenly he sensed someone else was in the room and turned. 'How the hell did you get in here?' he yelled at the six foot six, blond intruder facing him.

Albert made no reply, simply seating himself at the other side of Grant's desk.

'You cheeky son of a bitch,' raged Grant reaching for the panic button under his desk.

'Oh! Ja! I've immobilised it,' said Albert in even tones.

Adams stabbed at the button several times but with no effect.

'What do you want?' he said finally.

'Sorry about the entrance, Mr Adams, you have a very protective secretary,' said Albert extending his hand. 'I'm Albert Grossman. I work for Shell in The Hague. You may remember me from our meetings of eighteen months ago, about the joint venture.'

Adams relaxed a little but did not respond to the proffered handshake. 'Oh yes! I remember you,' he said, after a short pause. 'You're the clever son of a bitch who tried to outsmart me. Didn't get very far did you?' He swung back in his chair, clearly enjoying himself.

'You did, along with Shell, a good demolition job on me,' said Albert. 'You almost ruined my career.'

'No more than you deserved. You tried to rip us off. Come back for another go have you?'

'I'm here to make you an offer.'

A slightly bemused smile crossed Grant Adams' face. 'Well I give you this, you sure got balls . . . make it quick, I have to be away in a few minutes.'

'Must be the mistress tonight,' murmured Albert.

'Wha? What d'you say? How d'you know . . . ?'

'Never mind,' said Albert, 'in the interests of your flagging libido I'll cut to the quick.'

'Cheeky bastard!' yelled Adams rising from his desk.

'I'm here to save your business . . . at a price of course,' smiled Albert.

'Oh boy! You are really something, save my business eh! Are your brains in your clogs?' He waved a hand at a big screen hanging on the wall of his office which displayed the share prices of all the company stocks in real time. Everything was currently in green demonstrating continuous growth.

'What's to save?' he said with a coarse laugh.

'That can change very quickly,' insisted Albert.

Suddenly Grant's face became serious. 'What do you know?' he said, doubt suddenly clouding his mind.

'That the only part of your business which may be making money this time next year, is your sale of oil and gas for heating and power generation.'

'And why would that be so?'

'I have in my possession, an entirely different means of transportation, one that does not require oil, or its derivative products.'

'And what might that be pray?' said Grant, with a suspicion of a smile playing around the corners of his mouth.

'Matter transfer Mr Adams! I have the ability to move goods around the planet instantaneously without the need for your company product. I'm willing to cut you in on the deal, though God knows why, after the way you treated me.'

'What is this . . . Star Trek? Get out of my office boy, go stick your finger in somebody else's dyke,' snarled Adams suddenly, 'I don't do business with freaks.'

'Mr Adams, you need to be aware that with my technology I could bring your business to its knees, practically overnight. I'm offering you the opportunity to be in at the ground floor where you can make a killing over the rest of the oil industry. What I'm offering you will revolutionise world transport,' said Albert, ignoring the bluster from the older man. 'Allow me to demonstrate.'

Albert gritted his teeth and promptly disappeared, along with Grant's television set. After a brief pause the TV set reappeared at the other side of the room.

Grant Adams' eyes bulged and he began to shake with fear. He picked up the phone 'Security!' he yelled. 'Get me security, there's a nutter in my office!'

Albert reappeared, 'So you think I'm crazy do you?'

'Yeah! I'm having you arrested,' yelled Adams. 'Everyone will be safer when you're in the can.'

Now it was Albert's turn to shake, not with fear, but with rage. 'Unfortunately for you, Mr Adams, you can't keep me there can you? I'm giving you one last chance to take this seriously. I want half your business or I will destroy all of it.'

'Get out!' screeched Adams pointing at the door, 'I don't do business with lunatics and their cheap tricks.'

The office door crashed open and two uniformed security officers burst in. Adams spun around.

'Where is he?' yelled one, gun drawn and ready to deal with the incursion. Grant pointed over his shoulder at the empty room. 'There!' he shouted, 'Arrest him.'

The guards glanced at each other in surprise. 'But Mr Adams,' one said, 'there ain't nobody there to arrest.'

Grant Adams swung around only to find an empty space where Albert had been. 'Well he was here as sure as I'm talking to you, so go an' find him. He must still be in the building. You can't miss him, he's very tall and blond.'

The security guards backed out of the office giving each other sidelong glances as they went.

'Well that was exciting,' said Albert reappearing in Adams' plush office chair. 'Now let's have a look at your business?' he said pointing his smart phone at the screen on the office wall.

Grant Adams' jaw dropped as all the green indicators began to turn red, one by one progressively devaluing his company. He whipped around and made a lunge for the smart phone. Albert was too quick for him and disappeared, only to reappear on the other side of the room wearing a big grin. 'You haven't quite got it yet have you? Mr Adams, but you will; ja! You will.'

'It's just a trick. You're trying to scare me. All you're doing is changing that monitor with your gimmicky widget.

Well I promise you it won't work. I don't scare that easy.' He reached for the phone once more but it rang before he could touch it. He quickly slipped into his successful business man persona with a fixed smile on his face. 'Hi Alex, how are you today? Say again,' he said whipping around to observe the now completely red screen. 'But Alex, you can't do that!'

The line went dead, but as he replaced the receiver, it rang again and he was confronted by another upset investor. Meanwhile Albert was furiously operating his smart phone causing odd patches of the monitor to go green once more.

Adams spun around to confront the Dutchman. 'What the hell are you doing?' he screeched.

'It seems your investors are taking fright for some reason and I'm now buying your worthless stock,' grinned Albert. 'At a knock down price . . . of course. You would call that good business wouldn't you . . . Boy?'

At that moment the office door swung open to reveal Grant's secretary waving wildly. 'Mr Adams, the company Finance Director is on his way up to see you, something about a crisis run on your stock,' she wailed. Then she noticed Albert. 'How the hell did you get in here?' she cried.

'I would prefer you to address me courteously. Mr Grossman, if you don't mind,' said Albert.

'And why would I do that?' she responded, hands on hips.

'Because in a very few minutes, I will be your new boss,' said Albert, inspecting the screen closely, 'and my first task may be to fire you!'

The phone began to jangle once more, tearing at Grant Adam's nerves. He sat down at his desk with his head in his hands. 'What do you want me to do?' he groaned.

'Nothing!' said Albert curtly, 'It's too late now. You are no further use to me,' and vanished abruptly.

. . . .

Harry Fowler was in the queue at Kennedy Airport waiting to enter the departure lounge for Amsterdam, when his cell phone squawked. "Your man is in Houston causing mayhem and is being hunted by the FBI. You need to get to him before they do! A.P.", he read.

Turning away, he made his way quickly to the enquiry desk and re-booked his flight. Eight hours later he was standing in the blood splattered office of Grant Adams. To his practised eye the scene was a classic suicide, the gun still in the hand of the corpse slumped over the desk. His brains were splattered against the picture window, obliterating the splendid view of Houston. The FBI had interviewed Grant Adams' secretary and had found nothing to implicate Albert Grossman in his death, only the unexplained method of accessing him in his office. They had assumed this was a misunderstanding on her part and had not bothered to pursue it. Fowler suspected otherwise and carefully teased the truth out of the hysterical woman. The uniformed security guards confirmed his suspicions with their testimony. Albert Grossman had demonstrated the ability to appear and disappear at will in exactly the same way the captive teenagers had in Prague. As for the take over of the company stock, it appeared to the FBI that it had been bought legitimately, curiously however, at a ridiculously low price and with money that had been entirely borrowed. As the stock rose in value, the loan had been quickly repaid. All this had been done legally and, although they dearly wanted to interview Grossman, bringing a fraud charge without evidence would have been difficult. Houston was now buzzing with the news and crawling with FBI agents searching for Albert Grossman.

Harry Fowler checked into a hotel and phoned Alan Philby to confirm his worst fears. 'This guy can play the invisible man,' he growled, 'and the FBI's got nothing on him, not even breaking and entering. It seems he's somehow lifted the entire stock of Trust and now, in theory anyhow, owns the company, while the CEO's blown his brains out.'

'We have to get him somehow Harry. We can't let this thing hit the streets. You can imagine the panic it would cause.'

'Yeah, question is how, when he can just disappear if we approach him?'

Philby gave a dry cough. 'Do you think we could lay a trap by appealing to his vanity?'

'Perhaps,' said Fowler. 'I'll give it some thought. This Lucy Chu seems to be the key to everything, but like Grossman, she's impossible to pin down.'

'According to the two detectives investigating a gas explosion at the flat owned by Grossman's partner, both she and her mother are dead, and Grossman is firmly in the frame. It seems he stole the secret of the disappearing trick from her before he lit the fuse,' said Philby. 'So it looks like she has *been* pinned down, in a manner of speaking.'

'What makes them suspect Grossman?'

'They say they have an eyewitness account.'

'An eyewitness account to a gas explosion in a flat,' said Harry doubtfully, trying to visualise the circumstances which would allow the witness to escape unharmed and tell the tale later.

'Yes I understand your reluctance to go along with that, especially when the eyewitnesses are two phantasms inhabiting the programme we're trying to get our hands on.'

'Ah! Yes, I see,' said Fowler sarcastically. 'Like everything else on this case, that seems reasonable.'

. . . .

The Finance Director quickly established himself as acting CEO of Trust Oil and Gas and urged on by Harry Fowler, called an emergency board meeting to calm any fears of company collapse. Harry had insisted that the new owner of the company should attend, although how to contact this will o' the wisp was going to be a problem. Harry thought he may have resolved this by posting an invitation on the TV evening news channel along with the story of the unfortunate demise of Grant Adams.

When the directors assembled in the boardroom the following morning no one knew if this mystery man would turn up. They were aware, however, of three strangers in their midst, one of whom was Harry Fowler. There was some consternation at this intrusion, so the Finance Director attempted to settle the matter, explaining they were government officials from the audit office, who, in view of the unusual circumstances felt the need to oversee the transfer of the company to Albert Grossman. This went some way towards calming shattered nerves and the group settled down, with muted conversations, to await their new leader.

After an hour, they were just beginning to despair of Albert Grossman putting in an appearance, when the boardroom door swung open and the imposing, blond, handsome, figure swept in with a confident, 'Good morning gentlemen.' He stood at the head of the table and quickly surveyed the assemblage in front of him.

'I see we have three strangers with us today,' he began, 'they are welcome to witness the proceedings, whoever they represent.'

Harry Fowler started in astonishment, *How the hell does he know that, when all the people in the meeting are strangers to him?* He suddenly felt that all was not well and action should be immediate before Grossman became too suspicious and disappeared.

He gave a prearranged signal. The three outsiders jumped to their feet, pulled out guns, aimed at Albert, and simultaneously pulled the triggers of their Glock 19mm pistols.

CHAPTER 15

———•♦•———

Had it been possible Lucy would have had a wry smile on her face as she watched the scene unfolding in the Trust Oil and Gas boardroom. She quickly realised that Albert had done his homework and immediately spotted the three agents and particularly their guns. During his preamble he concentrated on the weapons and melted the muzzles, effectively blocking the bullet's exit. The three men had fired simultaneously and the result was mayhem. The guns exploded in their hands scattering high velocity metal fragments around the room. In the pandemonium that followed Albert vanished, but of particular interest to Lucy was the manner of his disappearance. She noticed he had gritted his teeth, as though operating a switch. Of course, she thought, this made it almost impossible for him to be caught, as the programmed response to this action was almost instantaneous. He had obviously perfected the method of using mobile phone and switch to good effect! To avoid being detected by Albert, she exited the scene immediately with a plan forming in her mind. *Maybe,* she thought, I *have found his Achilles heel.*

. . . .

Sophie stared in astonishment as Lucy appeared out of the portal. She reached out a hand and touched her on the arm. Lucy smiled. 'It's all right,' she said, 'I am real. Did you sleep well?'

She nodded. 'I think I was too exhausted to realise what was happening. How do you do that?' she said in halting English, pointing at the portal.

Lucy sat on Jack's bed alongside her. 'This is difficult to explain,' she began. 'Please understand that we didn't want this to happen, this was caused by Albert. We can teleport people through the portal.'

'How many of you can do this?'

'There are three of us and my father of course.'

'What happened to me?'

'I'll tell you what I think Albert did to you. First I must ask you, is he your lover?'

'Well,' she said, squirming slightly at the intrusion into her private life by this stranger, 'I suppose you could call him that.'

'My name is Lucy Chu. Does that mean anything to you?'

'Oh! You are Carla's daughter.'

'Well I was until Albert killed us both.'

'Yes, I remember now. Albert said Carla had had an accident, a gas explosion, I think.'

'That's right,' said Lucy carefully, 'except it wasn't an accident.'

'Just a moment, you said he killed you as well as your mother, but you are alive?' she said with a puzzled frown.

'My friend, Jack, rescued me just before the explosion. Unfortunately he was unable to rescue my mother.'

'I don't understand why Albert would do such a thing?' she said.

'Albert had discovered that we could teleport matter using a special computer programme and he wanted me to give it to him. He threatened my mother with death and so I had to give in. What I had not realised was that I was always going to be a threat to his ambitions, so . . .' she spread her hands in a gesture of acceptance, 'he never intended that I would survive, once he had the programme.'

'And your mother too?'

'Yes, because she was a witness.'

'And is she dead?'

'Yes.'

'Oh Lucy I am so sorry I had no idea he could be that evil. He could be very boring, always playing with his scientific things in that flat come laboratory. I hated it there. It made me feel used, so cheap and sleazy. Once we'd made love he had no further interest in me and went off to play with his toys.'

Sophie's confession tumbled out of her mouth unbidden, as though it had been festering for years. 'Do you remember anything of what happened to you?' said Lucy.

'Just been hit by this man, nothing else,' sobbed Sophie.

'Who was this man?'

'I think he was a client.'

'Client?' said Lucy her eyebrows arching in surprise, 'What sort of client?'

'I run an escort agency.'

'Oh I see. And do you know why this man hit you?'

'No! But why am I here, in England. How did I get here?'

Lucy nodded at the glowing orb in the centre of the room. 'Through the portal,' she said.

'I don't remember any of this,' she gulped. 'What happened to me?'

'We have an agent in Albert's laptop monitoring his actions. He told us that Albert had attempted to transport you to his flat, presumably after you were attacked. He used the programme to do this but, due to his inexperience, got it wrong. The result was your body was reassembled incorrectly. Mercifully you can't remember, because it wasn't pretty. I investigated and found you in Albert's flat, corrected his error and brought you back here where he can't harm you.'

Sophie stood up and walked around the portal slowly, trying to grasp what she had just being told. 'And so you put me back together in the right order?' she said finally.

'That's right.'

'So he wasn't even any good at science?'

'Unfortunately, he's getting better and becoming very troublesome.'

Sophie returned to the bed and sat alongside Lucy once more.

'I remember he said that he'd invented something and we were going to be very rich, is that it?' she said pointing at the portal.

'Invented?' gasped Lucy incredulously, 'Is that what he said? The nerve and conceit of the man! Well it seems he's using our programme to make mischief and in the process has alerted the CIA to the existence of the science my father and I have developed.'

'Where is your father?'

'He works for the physics faculty in a Chinese university. Where are your parents Sophie?'

'Oh, they're both dead,' she said sadly. 'They were killed a long time ago when I was about seven. A plane crashed on our flat in the outskirts of Amsterdam killing forty seven people.'

'Oh I'm sorry,' said Lucy. 'Do you have any relatives in Holland?'

'My aunt looked after my brother and me. He's a year younger than me. Now we seem to have drifted apart, but I still send him money . . . when I have some.'

'He's not working then?'

'No,' said Sophie, 'he's just come out of rehab' after his drugs problem. I think he's looking for a job now.'

'So how did you meet Albert?'

'We were at the same school. After the accident he used to look out for me. He was like an elder brother. We had things in common. His father was a brute who had walked out on his mother after beating her up. We supported each other in the difficult times.'

'And that carried on until you were both grown up?'

'Yes, I felt he was protecting me. I was fond of him but I was never in love with him. Had it been love I could never have started the escort agency. I was never sure about his feelings for me in that direction; I'm not convinced he could ever love anyone but himself. So the CIA is looking for him?'

Lucy nodded, aware that there could still be feelings for Albert in spite of the black picture she had painted.

'I don't understand,' she said, 'why are the Americans interested in a crime he committed in Holland?'

'They know he can do what we do and they're very nervous because they think he may be a terrorist.'

'What do you think?' asked Sophie.

'I think he's a murderer and a loner. He's not at all interested in any political dogma, unless you count selfishness in that,' said Lucy grimly. 'I wouldn't neatly parcel him up under the terrorist heading.'

'So what will they do to him if they catch him?' she said anxiously.

'Nothing compared to what I will do if I get to him first,' Lucy said bitterly.

Sophie fell silent, trying to reconcile her conflicting emotions; old loyalties to Albert and gratitude to her new friends, along with Lucy's grief at her mother's death at the hand of Albert.

. . . .

Jack was walking to his new digs in the centre of Cambridge, when he saw Megan coming towards him.

'Hi!' he said, 'Are you OK?'

'Yes I'm fine. Sorry about that outburst earlier. I didn't know what had happened. It's awful isn't it Lucy's mother being killed by Albert?'

'I only met him once,' said Jack. 'I must admit I didn't have him marked down as a murderer but I suppose it's the nature of the power Chu and Lucy have unleashed that turned him aggressive.'

'Don't start making excuses for him. It's a pity we can't put the genie back in the bottle,' she said despairingly.

'I know. I wished for an exciting life a year ago, but nothing like this. We've got ourselves in a bit of a pickle haven't we? And now the CIA's involved, of all things.'

'How did they find us Jack?'

'I don't know, but I suppose they're not going to give up until they get what they want.'

They walked into a café, sat down and ordered coffee. Megan pensively pushed a napkin around the table top.

'Where's it all going Jack?' she murmured. 'Will we ever get our lives back?'

He shrugged. 'Probably not the one you dreamed of, but at least it's not dull.'

'Have you thought perhaps the CIA should be told?'

'What do you mean?'

'At the moment Chu and Lucy are the owners of the programme and they owe allegiance to China.'

'We . . . ll, I don't know about that, Lucy's English.'

'Yes you do, we've talked about this before. In fact you once told me you'd had this conversation with Lucy when you first discovered what was going on.'

'Yes but . . .'

'Never mind *yes but*. Think about it; whoever has this programme has a massive advantage, and if it's China . . . ?'

'. . . We shouldn't be surprised that the CIA is interested?' He took a sip of coffee. 'You don't know that the Chinese have the programme. You're assuming that because Chu is Chinese and he works in China he has presented this science to the Chinese authorities. I don't know about you but when I was there I saw nothing to suggest he was being monitored or assisted by his government. I don't think they know what he's up to. If they did, he would be under lock and key!'

'Mmm, I suppose so . . . Is she? I never knew that, I just assumed she was Chinese,' said Megan.

Jack was temporarily mystified at this sudden turn in the conversation. Then he remembered the source of the detour she had just taken. 'As English as you and I. Probably more English than you because you claim to be Welsh.'

She gave him a hard stare then affectionately clipped him on the chin with her small fist. 'Jack Dawkins, sometimes I hate you!'

He smiled in return. 'Well I don't think *we* should hand it over to the CIA because it doesn't actually belong to us. It's for Lucy and Chu to decide.'

Megan rounded on him abruptly. 'And that's why I find you so infuriating and lovely at the same time,' she cried, rising from the table and heading for the exit.

'Wha?' he said in astonishment.

'You're so damn honest and naïve so you are,' she said, briefly kissing him on the cheek.

'But it's not *ours* to give away,' he protested.

They left the café, each with their private thoughts. 'What's Dipper doing there?' said Jack, suddenly.

'Oh don't worry about him, he's in seventh heaven. Chu seems to have adopted him as the son he never had and he's into everything Chinese, particularly the food.'

'The thing is,' said Jack thoughtfully, 'we don't really know what the Chinese intention is . . . but with Dipper on the spot . . . '

'. . . We might just find out,' finished Megan.

'Yes! What do you think?'

'He's a naturally nosey sod. Nobody better qualified in my opinion.'

'How do you feel about setting up a communication link with him?'

Megan paused on the pavement and screwed up her face in disgust. '"It is a far, far better thing that I do, than I have ever done",' she quoted.

'Alright don't get over dramatic about it, I'm not asking you to introduce yourself to Mme la Guillotine. If we find out that Chu's discovery is to be used against the West by the Chinese government, we need to talk with Lucy about it and decide between us what to do. Agreed?'

'I suppose so,' said Megan, resignedly. 'What about Albert?'

'I can't see him giving the CIA anything but trouble. Yes, he has to be stopped and I don't think Lucy needs any encouragement to deal with that. She's determined to get even.'

CHAPTER 16

Albert had occupied the luxury penthouse suite at the top of the Trust Oil and Gas building. No one within the higher echelons of the organisation had the nerve to challenge this, particularly after the attempted assassination. They were prepared to sit it out until the FBI decided what they were going to do. Meanwhile Albert examined the spectacular view from the top of what he considered to be his building and formulated a response to the CIA attempt on his life. He decided to research his adversary and called up the CIA website on his new laptop. He spent sometime familiarising himself with the headquarters layout at Langley, then switched his attention to the location of ICBM sites throughout the USA. Finally, he shut down the computer and wandered over to the picture window once more. He examined the rooftops of the surrounding skyscrapers, noting with interest the locations of the FBI snipers, who were there to pick him off if they got the chance. His face contorted into a twisted smile as an idea occurred to him. 'I suppose I can easily remove that threat completely,' he said.

Sitting down at the low coffee table he switched on the television and idly cycled through the enormous number of channels available. There was no mention of the failed attempt on his life by any of the news channels. 'They've hushed it up so that they don't look like fools,' he said to himself. 'Well they won't be able to hush up my retribution,' he chuckled.

. . . .

At the Minot Missile base in North Dakota, no one was aware that a Minuteman III missile had been stolen until it was generally announced that all silos around the United States should be inspected. The Facility Manager had done a swift investigation and confirmed that all the one hundred ton blast doors were in place and electronic interlocks were reading normally at the launch facility. It was only when the launcher support buildings were visually inspected that the loss was discovered and then all hell was let loose! The combat crew responsible for the missing missile huddled miserably in the launch control centre trying to understand the enormity of what had happened, while the Facility Manager was being interrogated on the phone by the Secretary of State for Defence.

'Mr Secretary,' he said, 'all the intruder alarms are showing normal readings, suggesting that the missile is in the silo. The blast door has not been removed and yet there is no missile in there. We can find no logical explanation for it. It should be impossible, and yet sir, there it is . . . gone!'

Some sixteen hundred miles away, in the lobby of the CIA Headquarters at Langley, the CIA badge set into the floor was partially obscured by the base of the miscreant Minuteman III, intercontinental ballistic missile. It had been painted from top to bottom in garish "dayglo" orange and a brief, but pointed message was inscribed on its side in precise lettering, "BANG! Welcome to my world." Underneath this in smaller script was written; "They seek him here, they seek him there,

The Yankees seek him everywhere.

Is he a man, is he a ghost?

The CIA *could* soon be toast!"

Upon its discovery, in the early hours of the morning, Alan Philby had wrestled with a difficult decision. If the missile warhead was armed he would have to evacuate the whole of Washington and probably everyone in a one hundred mile radius. If not, he still had to tell the President what had happened and that would undoubtedly have consequences. He was almost certain that this conjuring trick could only have been accomplished by one man and the message almost confirmed a non American was responsible. The orange colour was probably in celebration of the Dutch national football team. It was another demonstration of Grossman's ability to exercise formidable power, probably triggered by the failed assassination attempt, and left Philby with no choice other than to negotiate. That would have to wait. Right now he needed to know if the warhead was armed.

A helicopter roared down in front of the building and ejected its human cargo almost before the skids touched the tarmac. Six armed black suited individuals swarmed into the foyer, four assuming a guard at the base of the rocket while the other two erected a mobile gantry up to the nose cone of the missile. The decision came quite quickly and Philby breathed a sigh of relief as one of the armourers dropped an envelope down to him from the top of the gantry.

'Found that inside!' yelled the man. 'It's not armed!'

Alan Philby stood at the foot of the missile, coughed and scratched his head in bewilderment.

'Do you know where it's come from?'

The question was directed to the armourer who was descending from the warhead.

'Minot sir, North Dakota,' he grinned. 'I expect you were a little concerned. It's not every day one of these babies' lands in your back yard. You must have upset somebody real bad.'

'This is one son of a bitch we've got here,' breathed Jim O'Malley, appearing at Philby's side.

'Well, now we know what he can do,' replied Philby. 'But why? What's he after Jim?'

'Beats me,' said O'Malley, 'I guess he was just a little peeved because you tried to shoot him.'

'Well we can't go on like this. We have to take him seriously and find out what he wants.'

'Yeah!' agreed O'Malley, 'If one mad cloggy can do this, what can a billion chinks do?'

'Perhaps the answer's in here,' said Philby, ripping open the envelope.

He pulled out a short handwritten note. 'What's it say?' said O'Malley, anxiously.

Philby's pale face had turned grey with worry. 'He says that because he is operating at the quantum level of matter, he can short circuit all mechanical, electrical or electronic methods of safety interlocking, of not just this missile, but every missile, in every silo in the USA. He says he has arranged to automatically trigger all missiles should his own life be terminated by any future assassination attempt.'

He handed the note to O'Malley who re-read it slowly. 'My God!' he exclaimed finally, 'He's got our balls on a shovel.'

Alan Philby's cell phone jangled. 'Yes Mister President,' he said, 'it's safe, it was never armed. Yes Mister President, I'll be right there.'

. . . .

'He's been put under house arrest,' said Megan.

'Who?' asked Jack.

'Chu! The Chinese police arrested him last night and took him to a house in the outskirts of Shanghai. He has an armed guard posted outside his door permanently while the authorities are investigating him on a charge of spying.'

They were seated in the café once more, where Megan had arranged they should meet.

'Spying?' cried Jack incredulously. 'Who would Chu spy for, and why? It doesn't make sense. They should be treating him like a hero. He's spent most of his life producing a unique physics breakthrough which could have enormous benefits for mankind in general and the Chinese in particular, and his government's rejected it? I don't understand why governments behave like this,' he said, shaking his head in disbelief.

'Well I think there are two possibilities,' said Megan. 'The Chinese authorities recognise the potential of the programme but don't want Chu involved in its practical application, or they suspect they know what he's achieved and are now trying to make him confess.'

'I prefer the second explanation,' said Jack reflectively, 'Chu knows the danger of one super power having exclusive rights to the programme. Whether it's China *or* America, he knows it would lead to conflict. So he'll try to keep it secret from both until he thinks they're responsible enough to work in harmony with it.'

'If you're right, we need to get him out of that situation as soon as possible because they won't stop short at torture.'

'Come on!' said Jack, jumping to his feet, 'We need to see Lucy to find out where we should transport him to.'

As they headed back to the college, Jack said, 'What about Dipper?'

'Ah! Now here's the best bit, he's also locked up. Hopefully on a bread and water diet.'

'We'll have to get him out as well.'

'Can't we just leave him to starve . . . please?'

'We have to decide what to do with him . . . should we obliterate his memory?' said Jack, ignoring her comment.

'I'd feel better if we just obliterated *him*.'

'You don't mean that,' said Jack. 'He didn't ask to be interrogated by the CIA, or imprisoned by the Chinese.'

'He just happened to be in the right place at the right time,' said Megan, gleefully rubbing her hands.

'Have you no pity?' cried Jack.

'No! It's something to do with my gift for empathy which is more finely tuned to detect nonsense than yours.'

They reached Jack's old room, tapped on the door and walked in, startling Sophie who was brushing her teeth at the small sink in the toilet cubicle.

'Oh I'm sorry,' said Jack, noting the portal glowing in the centre of the room.

Sophie gingerly edged around it and sat on the bed. 'Lucy said she was going to find out what Albert is doing,' she said. 'What are you going to do with me?'

Megan looked puzzled. 'What do you mean?'

She gestured at the portal, 'I have seen what you can do and I know you want it kept secret, but you may not trust me to do that. You could kill me and nobody would know,' she sobbed.

'Now then darling,' Megan moved across to comfort her. 'Lucy didn't rescue you from Albert's cock up to do away with you.' Sophie wrapped her arms around Megan tightly and cried into her shoulder while Megan stroked her hair tenderly and murmured gently, 'Oh luvvy! Nobody's going to hurt you, I promise.'

The portal gave a gentle cough and Lucy appeared. 'Ah good,' said Jack. 'Now we're all here, we need to decide how to rescue Chu and Dipper.'

'Rescue Father, from what?' said Lucy, in surprise.

'He's under house arrest by the Chinese authorities,' said Megan. 'We need to work out a rescue plan. Unfortunately, it will have to include Dipper.'

. . . .

Jack transported himself to Lucy's room at Liverpool University, as they had agreed, and noted the shambles she had left behind when she had departed for Amsterdam. He switched on her laptop, quickly established the portal, pushed aside her clothes to make room for him to sit on her bed and waited. Lucy emerged first followed closely by Chu and then Dipper, looking nauseous. Megan had stayed in Cambridge to keep Sophie company.

'You once gave me a hard time for the state of my room,' Jack grinned, 'but at least you could see my bed.'

Lucy stuck out her tongue at him then seated her father on the only chair and gave him a quick cuddle. He returned the affectionate embrace. 'Thank you Jack for helping Lucy to rescue me,' he beamed. 'I'm sure they . . . ah . . . would have tortured me to death, for I would never allow the unworthy to have power and would not have given them information.'

'My pleasure,' said Jack. 'So nobody saw you, or the portal?'

'No, that was all pretty straightforward really. Getting Dipper out was a different story,' chuckled Lucy.

'Why, what happened?'

Dipper blushed self consciously.

'I'll tell you later,' she said winking. 'First I must tell Father that Albert Grossman has a copy of the programme and the password.' She told Chu what had happened at Carla's flat.

He was initially shocked and distressed at the news of his ex wife's demise but then said mysteriously, 'Don't worry Lucy, I fix.'

'You were right about American interest in what happened at Lichfield Crescent,' said Lucy. 'The CIA is desperate to understand what's going on, which is why they tried to interrogate Jack and Megan. Albert's made everything much worse now in America by taking over an oil company in Houston. The CIA tried to kill him. He escaped by operating a switch in his mouth which was wirelessly connected to his smart phone. I need to have the same facility Father, if I am to confront him.'

'He very dangerous man, you must be very careful. If Albert has done this, then so must we, but need access to . . . ah . . . laboratory.'

'That's not a problem,' said Lucy, 'we are in my room at Liverpool University. I thought you could renew your acquaintance with Gregory Harness and use the campus facilities.'

'Ah! Excellent idea! Then no problem to find suitably sized memory for your smart phone.'

'Good!' said Lucy. 'Now all we have to do is decide what to do with Dipper.'

Dipper was startled to be suddenly thrust into the discussion and was about to say something when he was interrupted by Lucy. 'The problem is, Father, he's seen everything we do. Perhaps we should erase his memory.'

Dipper's eyes suddenly seemed as large as saucers. 'What! You're going to turn me into a zombie?'

'I'm sure Megan would claim we don't need to do anything to achieve that,' chuckled Jack, mischievously.

'I have idea,' said Chu, quickly coming to the rescue. 'I need assistant while Lucy busy with Albert. I can use Dipper, he bright fellow . . . make good scientist.'

Dipper blushed and squatted on the floor. 'It would be amazing if I could stay here and work with Chu,' he agreed with a mixture of relief and excitement.

'Is that possible?' asked Lucy. 'I suppose *my* position here is still open, do you think Gregory would agree the swap?'

'I speak with him, but sure it will not be problem,' said Chu, winking at Dipper.

'That's settled then,' said Lucy.

'What happened with Dipper when you tried to get him out?' asked Jack.

Lucy chuckled. 'It seems that when the Chinese police came to the university to arrest Father, Dipper heroically tried to stop them. Obviously they noticed he was not Chinese and questioned his reason to be there. Suspecting him of spying, they decided to lock him up on campus while they continued their investigations. The only secure place they could find was a storeroom adjacent to . . . guess what?'

'The kitchen!' laughed Jack.

'When I established the portal in there, Dipper became hysterical. He thought the Chinese were going to transport

149

him to a labour camp away from all that lovely food. After I appeared, he calmed down a bit but still didn't want to leave. He only agreed to go when I told him we'd already rescued Father. Even then he resisted when I tried to bundle him into the portal. Fortunately no one came to investigate the howling and wailing coming from the storeroom before I was able close down the portal.'

Dipper sat on the floor squirming with embarrassment, and said nothing.

'It's just as well Megan wasn't involved,' said Jack, 'she would have left you there to rot.'

'I don't understand that girl,' said Dipper bitterly. 'Why does she insult me so much?'

'Maybe because you're an easy target,' said Jack, poking him in his ample stomach. 'In spite of the magnifying glasses you wear on your nose, you don't see it coming.'

'Come,' laughed Chu, motioning for Dipper to stand up, 'you and I go see Gregory and make the arrangements.'

When they had left, Jack paced around the room restlessly.

'Ok, what is it?' said Lucy, noting his discomfort.

'I don't like you going after Albert like this . . . on your own and without a proper plan.'

'I'll be fine,' she protested. 'I'll have the same means of escape as Albert after Father has programmed my smart phone.'

'Mm,' said Jack doubtfully, 'perhaps I should go with you.'

'This is my revenge, not yours,' she cried, indignantly, '*I* will avenge my mother's death!'

Jack was shocked at the vehemence of her response. 'Lucy, I would have saved her if it was possible,' he protested, guiltily.

She gave him a stony glare, 'Go back to Cambridge Jack; this is *my* affair.'

Jack whispered, 'Good luck!' as he stepped into the portal. He knew he would never persuade her to allow him to help.

CHAPTER 17

———————————•❦•———————————

Simply thinking of Albert transported her to his location in the penthouse flat on the top floor of the Trust Oil & Gas offices. The FBI and CIA were aware of his occupancy but had temporarily given up trying to catch him there. The CIA in particular had now re-grouped to nurse their wounded pride and work out a new strategy which would not bring ridicule down on their heads.

Albert whistled softly to himself as he stood in the shower. All was going to plan. Whatever they had thrown at him had been ineffective. He was beginning to show them that he was a force to be reckoned with. The nuclear missile stunt had really driven home the message, although he had never intended to arm it. It would certainly have been possible by working at the atomic level, to have by passed all the safety features and armed the missile. Now they had seen what he was capable of they had to take him seriously and the next part of his plan required that they should.

He didn't think that Chu was providing his technology to the Chinese authorities. Conversations with Carla had convinced him that Chu was totally non political and would resent that type of interference in his work.

As he reached for the towel and began to dry himself, he froze and strained to hear a movement in the lounge, sensing he was not alone. *Perhaps moving in other dimensions sharpened the senses in this one* he thought. Whatever, someone was in the lounge area. *My phone*! He'd left it on the coffee table while he showered. *Stupid mistake*! he chastised himself, as he dressed hurriedly. Slamming open the bathroom door, he was confronted by Lucy, his phone innards in one hand and its memory card in the other!

Rapidly recovering from the initial shock he growled, 'You're supposed to be dead.'

'And you're supposed to be the protector of my mother, and look what you did to her . . . and to me!' she spat out.

'Ja! Just goes to show doesn't it, you can't take anything for granted. Why didn't you die? This just means I'll have to kill you all over again.'

'Well maybe,' said Lucy, 'but at least you won't have this any more.'

She held the memory card between finger and thumb, popped it into her mouth, and swallowed it. He made no move to stop her but smiled evilly. She realised why he was remaining calm when he pulled from his pocket an identical card.

'Now it would have been very silly of me wouldn't it, had I not made several copies?' he said. She suddenly realised the danger she had placed herself in and made a dash for the door. Albert threw out a restraining arm and caught her wrist, clamping his big fingers around it. She screamed in pain as he forced her arm up her back.

'Now I have you,' he barked, pushing her towards the door leading onto the roof. Opening it with his free hand he shoved her roughly outside. 'It seems such a shame to kill somebody like you,' he snarled. 'You could be so useful to me. How would you like to join me, we could work together on my project? Together we would be invincible.'

'You killed my mother,' she gasped as the pain filled her arm and shoulder. 'I can't even live on the same planet as you.'

'Very well, you leave me no choice. I can't afford to have you opposing me all the time. Say whatever Buddhist prayers you have in that stupid, stubborn head, because this time you *will* die.'

He pushed her across the roof until they reached the safety rail at the edge of the seventy story sheer drop. He momentarily released her arm and grabbed her around the waist. Lucy struggled and tried to claw at his eyes but he was far too strong for her. He lifted her bodily over the rail then let go of her with a sardonic, 'Bye bye!' She screamed and her hands flailed out, one clamping around the rail, her legs dangling in free space. She pulled out her smart phone with her free hand. With an exultant cry Albert crashed his big fist onto her tiring fingers, again and again until they released their grip and she dropped out of sight.

. . . .

Collins and Van Penn were blindfolded and dumped in the back of the limousine once more. Neither man spoke, each being suspicious of what the other had revealed in the short interrogation. The limousine sped through the outskirts of Prague and then went uphill for a short distance. At least they weren't destined for a river thought Collins with some relief. The car described a short turning circle and stopped abruptly. For a moment there was silence. The rear door was opened and a voice said, 'Stay there while I remove blindfolds and tie-wraps.'

As his blindfold was removed, Collins peered out of the open door and was startled to see several men in pale blue military uniforms march past in perfect synchronism, arms swinging and rifles at the slope. He blinked in confusion. Where was this? It didn't look much like Egypt.

'Get out,' said Joseph. 'Enjoy your holiday. You're tourists now, but remember, we know where to pick you up again. Nothing of this must appear in your reports.'

He drove off, leaving Collins and Van Pen disorientated, in an enormous grey, cobbled square surrounded by large pale yellow, stone buildings and hundreds of camera clicking Japanese tourists. Collins peered at the building in front of him and its magnificent wrought iron, black painted gates topped with gold painted floral designs, glinting in the morning winter sun. The gate walls were adorned with heroic carvings depicting some kind of sacrificial killing on one side and an eagle supported by cherubs on the other. Behind the gates was the magnificent edifice of what looked like a royal palace. He turned around and looked at the opposite side of the square where the spires of an enormous cathedral could be seen peeping over the top of a row of unremarkable squat, office like buildings. He spread his hands in despair and turned to Van Penn. 'Where the hell are we?'

'I wouldn't have expected a part time European like you to know,' he sneered. 'We're in Praha.'

'Where?'

'Prague, in your terminology,' Van Penn responded.

'We have to have a look around that fantastic cathedral.'

'I think the CIA's addled your brain. We're not here to go sightseeing,' said Van Penn scathingly.

'Well . . . no, but I thought while we have the chance . . .'

'Come on, we have a train to catch,' said Van Penn.

'Train?' said Collins vaguely.

'Wake up! Yes, train to Amsterdam!'

'But Joseph said we should be tourists.'

Van Penn eyed him disbelievingly. 'And you really thought that's what he meant?'

'Well . . . er . . . yes.'

Van Penn turned sharply on his heel and began walking down the hill towards the river with Collins reluctantly trotting along behind him. 'It doesn't say much for your police force that *you* became a Detective Sergeant,' he said.

'Well at least I didn't tell the CIA anything. Did you?'

'Very little.'

'They told me that you were very co-operative. You told them everything, didn't you?'

'Not everything.'

'What did they threaten you with to get you to talk?'

'Nothing! I . . .'

'So you just blurted it all out, like a naughty child? It must be easy work for your police force if all Dutchmen confess before they're even questioned.'

'This!' said Van Penn, trying to change the subject, 'Is the Charles Bridge, across the river Vitava.'

Collins was not to be deflected. 'I bet you gave them a good laugh with wild stories of a talking paper clip, didn't you?' he insisted.

'I told them what we'd seen in Grossman's flat. They didn't seem at all surprised by it.'

'Doesn't that strike you as rather strange, almost as though they expected something like it?'

'Well er . . . yes . . . I suppose so. So what did *you* tell them?'

'Absolutely nothing,' said Collins, haughtily. 'They knew that we had found the DVD containing the programme they were looking for, but obviously it wasn't in our possession when they kidnapped us.'

'And I suppose they searched the flat and couldn't find it there either,' said Van Penn.

'Did you tell them that it had ejected itself from the laptop and disappeared into the bedroom?' asked Collins accusingly.

'Well yes, but I think you told the Deputy Director it was somewhere in the bedroom when he phoned you . . . didn't you?'

'I may have done I can't remember,' said Collins ruefully. 'Does it matter?'

'Probably not, I expect they realised they wouldn't get anything sensible out of the village idiot,' sneered Van Penn.

The bickering pair continued across the river and into Wenceslas square before turning off towards the railway station.

'Two singles to Amsterdam,' said Van Penn to the railway ticket clerk.

'Will that be a double cabin?' queried the clerk.

'No! Two singles,' cut in Collins quickly.

'Definitely!' agreed Van Penn.

'Worth every penny of the extra,' said Collins as they searched out the platform.

'Unfortunately, we have been put at the same end of the train,' said Van Penn.

'Being on the same train's bad enough,' said Collins.

They sat together in the waiting room later sipping coffee. 'So what are you going to say in your report?' said Van Penn. 'How are you going to account for the missing day and the expenses claim for the ticket from Prague to Amsterdam, bearing in mind there's no equivalent ticket from Amsterdam to Prague?'

'You've met Smiley, how do you think she would take the truth?'

'She'd think you'd been on holiday at police department expense. My boss would be the same.' He paused reflectively. 'I think we'd better make up some innocent story and both stick to it.'

'How can I trust you to do that? You're obviously a blabbermouth,' said Collins. 'Any sort of pressure and it all comes tumbling out.'

'Look! We have to agree on this or we're both sunk,' said Van Penn miserably. 'I don't like trusting you anymore than you like trusting me. Do we have a deal?'

He extended his hand across the table and Collins took it. There was that limp handshake again. 'Deal!' sighed Collins reluctantly.

As the train pulled into Amsterdam the following morning they had finally agreed on the report they would each file in their respective departments. There was no mention of paper clips, butlers, disappearing DVD's or extraordinary rendition by the CIA. Their bland reports effectively put the whole investigation of the death of Lucy Chu and her mother in the temporarily suspended folder, pending further investigation. Collins remained troubled by the CIA involvement, which was probably triggered by the police report into the strange happenings concerning Lucy Chu. He was also irritated that everyone who had an interest, seemed to have a copy of the report, except himself . . . the co-author!

. . . .

Harry Fowler looked down at the body of the girl at his feet. He had, in his career, seen a few suicides involving tall buildings, bridges and the like, but nothing ever like this. Enough of her face was exposed to confirm that she was of Chinese origin; that was straightforward enough, what concerned him most was the lack of damage to her body. Everything appeared to be unharmed, no blood, bruising or broken bones. You could almost expect that at any moment she would stand up and walk away as if nothing had happened. It was as though she had simply appeared there, rolled over and gone to sleep and yet, there were witnesses who all agreed she had fallen from the top of the seventy story high building. Furthermore, witnesses also agreed that she was fully clothed, and yet this girl was completely naked. Harry scratched his head and squatted down to check her pulse once more to confirm she was not alive. He pulled the sheet back over her lifeless form and straightened up, then peered up at the top of the Trust Oil & Gas building where he knew Albert Grossman had taken up residence and claimed ownership of the company. The legality of that was still being fiercely contested. The CIA had posted cameras up there on adjacent buildings to keep a watch on their slippery adversary. 'That should show what happened,' he murmured to himself, as he eased his right arm into a more comfortable position in the sling around his neck. The other agents had fared little better after their failed attempt to gun down Grossman and several board members had suffered minor shrapnel wounds from one of the guns which had exploded. Fowler was still intrigued as to how Grossman had known the agents had guns and how he had caused them to explode. Ballistics had suggested that the gun muzzles had been welded up . . . but how?

The photographs having been taken, the police left the body in charge of the ambulance crew for transport to the morgue and post mortem, while Fowler was left wondering what it was going to take to stop the man living at the top of the building above him.

Later, at CIA headquarters in Langley, he scanned the available video footage until he found the part he was looking for. The video cameras showed quite plainly what had happened. In fact Grossman had actually waved a greeting at them after tipping the girl off the roof and returning to his penthouse suite. 'The arrogance of the man's breathtaking,' growled Fowler to his colleague, Perrin.

Perrin grimaced. 'Well at least we know he did it. Problem is, how can you catch the bastard?'

'I suppose the snipers could pick him off when he appears,' said Fowler, without much conviction.

'I think you need to get him alive,' said Perrin.

'Why? He deserves a bullet in his head. Look at what he did to that poor girl, and then he has the nerve to wave at the camera.'

'But if you kill him, how are we ever going to find out how he manages to perform these miracles?' persisted Perrin. 'Anyway, a little bird tells me he's booby trapped his own body.'

'What do you mean?'

'One of the snipers told me they've been instructed not to shoot him.'

'Why?'

'I don't know any more than that,' said Perrin, holding up his hands to ward off further enquiry.

'This makes it doubly difficult,' said Fowler thoughtfully. 'I need to check this out with Philby.'

'Do we know yet who this girl was?' said Perrin.

'No! Come on let's go and see how the autopsy's going,' said Fowler, grabbing his coat.

. . . .

She tumbled over head first and saw the drop facing her. Fighting against the fierce slipstream as she gathered speed, she tried to focus on the keypad of her smart phone. Her eyes were watering making it almost impossible to see the keys clearly. She desperately tried to select the shortcut button Chu had set up. 'Where's the key?' She yelled, as the ground came rushing up to meet her. At the top of the building, Albert leaned over the handrail and watched Lucy's slight figure disappear into the grey haze below. He smiled with satisfaction, then quickly slipped into the office behind.

Chu had programmed Lucy's smart phone with two shortcut keys, one to initiate teleportation and the other to enable a copy of herself to be produced. He had previously produced a copy of Lucy when the police had attempted to deport her to China with him, so for him, this was a simple task. A matter of milliseconds before impact with the pavement, Lucy managed to press both keys simultaneously. This resulted in the copy being produced without the kinetic energy of the original. The copy flopped onto the sidewalk from a few inches above causing no damage, while Lucy was immediately transported into the world of pure energy. She considered whether to return to do battle with Albert then dismissed the idea. She would have to find an alternative way, one from which he could not escape. Thinking of Jack, she was transported back to Cambridge and his student room, where he welcomed her warmly.

'You were right,' she admitted, 'he's made copies of the programme, so stealing one didn't help.'

'You've stolen one. Where is it?' said Jack, excitedly.

Lucy pointed dumbly at her stomach.

'You swallowed it?'

Lucy nodded.

'So we have to wait until . . . ?'

She nodded again.

'And then we have to . . . ?'

A thin smile played around her lips. 'Well, you will help me won't you Jack?'

It was his turn to nod, 'I suppose so,' he said, resignedly.

'So why do you think it will help?'

'If it came out of his smart phone, it must contain his DNA.'

Lucy's eyes widened with understanding as she realised what he was implying. 'Relax,' she grinned, 'I know where the memory card is and I have to remove a mistake from the morgue anyway.'

Jack, mystified, watched her disappear once more into the portal.

. . . .

'This is the strangest case I have ever seen,' said the pathologist, brandishing his scalpel. 'How do you guys think she died?'

Fowler looked puzzled. 'High velocity impact with the sidewalk?' he guessed.

'Wrong!' said the pathologist emphatically. 'She was never alive in the first place.'

'But we have video footage of her assailant throwing her off the top of the building, and believe me she was alive then, she was fighting for her life.'

'Well this,' he waved a casual hand at the corpse on the table, 'never was.'

'How can you be so sure?' interjected Perrin.

'Because she was constructed, and some vital parts are missing.'

'Such as?' said Fowler.

'There's no blood and stomach acid for a start. This girl's never had a meal in her life. The only thing that's ever been in her stomach is this.' He held up a tiny object in his tweezers for their inspection.

'It's a memory card out of a smart phone.' said Perrin. He peered at it closely. 'One hundred and twenty eight gigabytes, that's some memory.'

'Was that the only thing in her stomach?' said Fowler.

'Yes.'

Suddenly Harry Fowler's mind went back to the original briefing with the CIA Deputy Director when he presented the British police report concerning Lucy Chu. 'We've been here before,' he muttered. 'I wouldn't mind betting that this body, if that is what it is, will disappear.'

'So if this . . . thing was never alive, there can't have been a murder,' said Perrin.

Fowler looked at him curiously for a moment then turned to the pathologist. 'Have you taken a DNA sample?'

'First thing we did,' he replied.

'OK we need to check it out against some information we have which might give us a clue to her identity, but my money's on Lucy Chu. This is a copy of Lucy Chu,' he said emphatically, pointing at the body. 'This!' he turned around and held the memory card under a desk light at the side of the room, 'Is the programme we're looking for.'

He turned the card over between his fingers to examine the other side and they all bent over to inspect it more closely. Then it disappeared!

'What the hell!' cried Perrin. 'Where'd that go?'

Fowler turned to examine the floor behind him thinking he may have dropped the card. 'Oh shit!' he cried, pointing at the empty slab, 'She's gone!'

CHAPTER 18

———•—•———

Alan Philby was ushered into the Oval office by an aide to await the audience with Rick Newman, the U.S. President. He was very concerned as his performance of late had not been good, thanks mainly to the antics of the Dutchman, Albert Grossman. Rick Newman was renowned for his habit of arbitrarily dismissing employees while allowing no leave of appeal. This had earned him the nickname of "Bullit Newman". It was wise therefore, to always agree with his comments regardless of their veracity. Alan Philby was well aware of this and was very much on his guard.

Rick swept in, popped a jelly bean in his mouth, and offered one to Philby from a crumpled paper bag he kept in his pocket. Philby politely refused. Rick eased his slightly overweight body into the chair behind his desk and treated Alan, to his characteristic, expectant, toothy, campaign grin, which seemed to say, 'What yer gonna do fer me?'

'Now Ira whatcher got fer me?' He was in a good humour, and clearly only wanted to hear favourable news. Philby realised it would not be a good idea to correct the misunderstanding of his name. If the President said so, he was now, "Ira".

'Well sir we've been having a problem with this Dutchman.' he began tentatively.

The President finger flicked a golf ball and exclaimed loudly as he missed some self declared, target on the vast expanse of his desktop.

'A Dutchman you say?'

'Yes sir.'

'How do I get "dutchland" on this computer?' he said, glaring at the screen and occasionally prodding a key.

Philby suppressed his anxiety and moved behind Newman to assist with the search on Google earth, finally bringing up The Netherlands on screen. The President screwed his face up in disgust. 'Well hell Ira, that ain't no bigger than a golf course. You sure that's a whole country?'

'Yes sir, with its own royal family.'

'No! You serious? How comes a country that size gets a royal family? Don't seem right!'

Philby made a desperate attempt to bring the conversation back to the issue which was concerning him. 'This Dutchmen has taken over the Trust Oil & Gas Company in Houston,' he ventured.

'Is it ligit?'

'We're not sure sir; the FBI is investigating. It seems he was able to illegally manipulate the "Dow Jones" in some way.'

'Nothing wrong there Ira, how the hell d'ya think I got rich?'

'We also suspect he's wanted for murder in Europe.'

'Has he committed any crimes here?'

'Nothing that we can prove,' said Philby.

'Sounds like he should be on my campaign team,' joked the President. 'With the upcoming election we could sure use slippery people like that.' His attention wavered once more as he fingered his computer keyboard. 'Y'know Ira, once I get the hang of this thing, I should be able to do your job as well as mine. I'm told you can get everything off the internet, you just have to go onto something called, "Wiki leaks" and it tells you everything you need to know. So why do we need another intelligence agency?'

Philby coughed and almost choked, wondering whether the President's strange sense of humour was at play, or if he was indeed serious. He decided it would be best to ignore his bizarre behaviour. 'Well the thing is sir he seems to have special powers.'

'Special powers eh? What yer mean like "Superman"?'

'Well not quite like that sir, his abilities are based on a real scientific discovery. Something we've been working on for almost three decades.'

'Are you saying this guy's got the drop on the whole scientific community in the USA?'

'Unfortunately it looks that way sir.'

The words hung in the air and the President remained immobile for several seconds. Philby was startled by the nature of the explosion when it finally came. Rick Newman reached out and picked up his phone, scowled, and rang the Head of the Infrastructure Financing Authority. 'Suspend all finance to the scientific community as of now,' he yelled. 'I'm not paying these morons to let themselves be trumped by some small time conjurer from a two bit country . . . with a royal family.' He slammed the phone down and smiled at Philby, 'I prefer "Batman" myself; he drives a flashy car, if yer know what I mean.'

Once more Philby's mind slipped down a gear to grapple with the situation. 'Well this guy managed to transport an ICBM into Langley headquarters.'

'Oh yeah, I remember now, that's why I wanted to talk with you. Now that's bad Ira, that's real bad. Now yer shouldn't be letting that sort o' thing happen. It's bad fer my publicity yer understand. Yer gonna have to nail that guy an' quick.'

'Yes sir, unfortunately his special powers enable him to avoid arrest.'

'Hell Ira, yer've got the biggest budget in the whole of this great country of ours. Have yer any idea how much I struggle every year to git yer budget through Congress? Can't yer just export the bastard back to where he belongs?'

'No sir, it's impossible to catch him, he just keeps disappearing, and he's rigged the whole of our nuclear arsenal so that if we manage to kill him every ICBM in the country will explode.'

'Funny you should say that Ira, but ma 'lectric razor dang disappeared this mornin', can yer imagine that? Thought I might have to go to work covered in unsightly stubble. Bad fer the image yer know 'ticularly in election year. Anyways it turned up exactly where I left it, strange eh!'

'Yes sir, anyway as I was saying, this guy is able to disappear and appear again anywhere he likes.'

'Bit like the invisible man?' offered the President.

'Yes something like that,' said Philby, desperately struggling to make a connection.

'That's easy then, jus' look fer the bandages, then yer got yer man,' joked Newman. 'Now Ira you just get yer arse back to Langley and sort this out, I can't afford to have some foreigner spraying live ICBM's around the country . . . in an election year.'

'Yes sir.'

'And Ira.'

'Yes sir?'

'Yer don't look well. Get yerself some medical advice!'

. . . .

Alan Philby called an emergency meeting to discuss the latest developments and dispel any rumours regarding the competence of the CIA after the missile incident. He gave a brief preamble to that effect.

Mary Cairns, clearly agitated, challenged Philby head on, her face crumpled with anger. Her eyes bored in to the director's. 'We are a laughing stock,' she complained loudly. 'So much for security, this place has more holes in it than a colander. How can I explain a Minuteman missile appearing in the forecourt to my people? Have you any idea what this has done to morale?'

'Mary, we all feel the same way but this guy has powers which are way beyond our control.'

'And what have you done about it?'

'Look I've asked you here today to bring you up to date with the problem we are facing and I would be grateful for any suggestions you may have to resolve the issue. I feel you need to be made aware of all the facts first. I do understand your anger, but we must keep a clear, collective mind to bottom this out,' said Philby, desperately trying to maintain his authority.

'I hope you're not going to give us that, "thinking outside the box" crap,' said Jim O'Malley.

'Jim, just calm down and let's hear what Harry can tell us first.'

Harry Fowler gave the group a brief run down on what had occurred since their last meeting. There were suffused sniggers when he explained the reason for the sling to those who were unaware of the failed attempt on Grossman's life. This was quickly tempered by the realisation of what Grossman could do.

'I suppose he was a bit upset that you tried to blow him away, hence the missile,' said O'Malley.

'I'm sure he never intended to set it off. He just wanted to scare us,' interjected Philby.

'Well that bit sure as hell worked,' agreed Mary waspishly.

Harry went on to describe the events in the mortuary and the group became silent while trying to absorb the bizarre happenings.

'How do you know this . . . this copy was Lucy Chu?' asked Barry Martinez.

'I didn't at the time. I just suspected it was after I remembered the British police report. We checked the DNA with that of Lucy Chu later and it proved to be an absolute match.'

'So this girl, copy, or whatever, crashed into the sidewalk at something like one hundred miles per hour and received no physical injuries. How do you explain that?' asked Jim O'Malley.

'I can't,' said Harry simply.

The group were silent while they tried to come to terms with this new, impossible, piece of physics.

'So you say Grossman was video'd throwing her off the building, presumably kicking and screaming but according to the pathologist she was never alive?' said Martinez.

'That's pretty much what he said.'

'So how do you charge a guy with murder when the victim was never alive?' added Martinez.

Fowler shrugged his shoulders in response.

At this point Philby interceded. 'We are pretty sure that the memory chip taken from her stomach was the programme we've been trying to get. Someone, or something, didn't want that chip to fall into our hands and made it disappear.'

'Disappear uh! Just like magic?' said Mary with a disbelieving frown. 'So if the body on the sidewalk was a copy of Lucy Chu, where's the original?'

'Look,' protested Harry, 'I'm just telling it how it was. I have nothing to gain by telling you fairy tales.'

'OK Harry,' said Philby, 'nobody's suggesting you're embroidering the truth, and in answer to your question Mary, she's supposed to be dead. That's why there are two foreign sleuths plodding around Europe, investigating her murder.' He recounted the story of Collins and Van Penn and how the DVD had mysteriously disappeared.

Jim O'Malley's exasperated eyes rolled skywards and he belched loudly. 'They were in Grossman's flat when all this happened and they saw a talking, walking, paper clip, who claims he witnessed the murder of Lucy Chu and her mother?' he said.

'Yes,' said Philby. 'We questioned Van Penn at great length. He seemed like an altogether guy, but yes, he came out with this strange tale.'

'And was it corroborated by his sidekick, Collins?'

'No, he refused to speak to us about it.'

There was a long pause during which time everybody took a drink of water as if to fortify themselves against any more incredible revelations and O'Malley's halitosis. Muted conversations began around the table.

'Is that it Alan?' said O'Malley.

'Yes . . . except I managed to have a telephone conversation with Grossman.' Suddenly he had everyone's attention again. 'And this is a recording of it.'

He pressed a button on the desk and the phone could be heard ringing.

'Ja!' said Grossman.

'Mr Grossman?' said Philby, 'This is Alan Philby, CIA Deputy Director.'

'Ah! Ja!' said Grossman, 'I have been expecting you to call. How did you like my little gift in your entrance hall?'

'It caused a lot of inconvenience I'm afraid.'

'Small price to pay for the inconvenience you nearly caused me.'

'OK, I take your point Mr Grossman, but perhaps you can understand our concern when you take over one of our major oil companies overnight and the CEO commits suicide?'

'Mr Philby, I gave the man every opportunity to join me in my little venture, but he was . . . shall we say . . . less than enthusiastic . . . almost insulting.'

'Is that any reason to drive the poor man to commit suicide?'

'That was his choice.'

'Mr. Grossman, I think we should resolve our differences before someone else gets hurt, don't you?'

'I would prefer to work with you,' retorted Grossman.

'Was your takeover of Trust Oil and Gas, fraudulent?'

'You have a strange way of resolving differences, Mr. Philby, however I would admit to manipulating the market a little. Isn't that what Wall Street does every day. I don't make the rules; I simply choose to benefit from the absurdity of them.'

'Ok, so what do you want?'

'I repeat, I would prefer to work with you rather than against you, but unfortunately in America, you have a habit of destroying what you do not understand. This I believe is born out of fear. A strange paradox don't you think, Mr Philby, for a nation supposed to be the most powerful on earth? You proclaim your particular type of freedom as desirable, something the rest of the world should emulate and yet, one insignificant person can cause so much angst and fear. This suggests instability in your structure. Is it your desire to inflict this neurosis on the rest of the world's population in order that *you* can feel more comfortable with it?'

'We have to protect our interests,' said Philby, feebly trying to avoid the philosophical discussion.

'Regrettably you are too immature to properly understand what your interests are, which is why I cannot allow you to have the programme you are so desperate to own. It would be like giving a ten year old child a machine gun for Christmas and telling him to go out and enjoy himself.'

'But the Chinese already have the technology . . . we must preserve a balance,' protested Philby.

'Do they? Are you sure? I suggest you are allowing your fear to dictate to your intelligence.'

'What do you mean?'

'How much do you know about the inventor of the programme, his daughter and their relationship with the Chinese government?'

'Only what we gathered from the British police report.'

'And based on that, you believe the Chinese nation is about to use this science to ruin your country! What kind of intelligence agency are you running there Mr Philby? I lived with the inventor's ex wife for nearly four years and learned a lot about him during that time. While I admire him as a brilliant scientist, it was clear to me that he is totally naïve when it comes to world politics. He will never give anything away to the Chinese authorities. So mistrusting is he that he would cheerfully die to retain his integrity and the secret of his programme. So you see Mr Philby you have made ill informed judgements and acted irrationally upon them. Now you expect me to work with your appalling unprofessional behaviour. But then, I suppose that's the American way, and you are not to be blamed for the culture which raised you. However, you should bear some responsibility for improving it as a mature adult. You are mature are you not?'

'I try to be,' said Philby, reeling from the unexpected abuse, 'but I repeat, what do you want?'

'I am sure neither Mr Chu, nor I would want to suffer the same fate as your Mr Oppenheimer when he uttered those famous words after the test of the first atom bomb, "Now, I am become Death, the destroyer of worlds".'

'What has that to do with this?' said Philby, worried where this bizarre conversation was leading him.

'With those words he took responsibility upon himself which was not his. The authorities were more than happy for him to do it, for it absolved them, as they thought, from any responsibility for subsequent events. *He* did not become death, *they* did. It's quite easy to blame other people for your mistakes when you are in power, is it not Mr Philby? Another famous wartime leader referred to "the lights of perverted science". Science is a search for truth. It cannot be perverse in itself. It can however be perverted by those who seek to make personal gain from its implementation. It is relevant because given the opportunity you would use this science for political ends. You and your society will always behave in this way and you therefore cannot be trusted to act in a mature way . . . for the good of society.'

'That's as maybe, but what is it you are after?'

'You see, Mr Philby you dismiss the argument with a "that's as maybe" and will not involve yourself in a sensible discussion on the subject. Regrettably, with that attitude, you deserve the society you are building. The science is there, you have witnessed it for yourself. Like nuclear fission, it will not go away. The question now is how to deal with it.'

'Agreed,' said the Deputy Director, relieved to find some common purpose at last. 'But why should you be involved? What's so special about you that you need to be part of the solution?'

'Left to your own devices, you would further the interests of America to the exclusion of the rest of the world. Sufficient evidence of that exists in the oil industry alone. China, or Russia for that matter, would do the same. I represent the ordinary man, from a very minor country, which has no desire to dominate on the world stage. I am the ideal person to oversee the introduction of this technology for the benefit of *all* mankind and should therefore have the ultimate say in its use . . . or not.'

'And yet, were you to be granted this power, you *would* dominate,' interrupted Philby.

'That's true, but not from your position of fear and self interest, that is the crucial difference. I already have that power, for I can place *armed* missiles anywhere around the world. I don't need your permission, nor would I ever seek it, for I believe you are not competent to make any judgement. Imagine the reaction of the Kremlin if an American missile turned up in Red Square.'

'You wouldn't do that,' protested Philby, in alarm.

'Probably not, because I am prepared to exercise the responsibility that goes with the power, whereas you . . .

with your "if I don't understand it . . . kill it", policy . . . ?
Well who knows? But remember, undetected by your
security arrangements, I can be anywhere at any time. Even
your President is not safe! Well I'll let you get back to your
meeting now Mr Philby. I'm sure you have a lot to discuss,
cheerio.'

The members of the meeting sat in silence for a few
moments absorbing what had been said, bewildered by the
inadequacy of their leader and also his apparent willingness
to reveal it. Martinez broke the silence. 'I thought you said
that telephone conversation was a recording.'

'It was . . . from about two hours ago.'

'So how did he know we were having a meeting . . .
now?'

Philby was about to speak, then paused as he realised
what Martinez was implying, 'I guess he's right here,
now . . . we just can't see him,' he said slowly.

'Are we to presume then that he is watching our
deliberations and listening to everything we say?' said
Mary.

'I think we have to,' said Philby.

The group fell silent.

Albert chuckled softly to himself. 'So much for
security.'

CHAPTER 19

Albert had to admit it to himself . . . he was lonely! It was all very well having the trappings of an opulent lifestyle, he reasoned, but he needed to share it with someone, someone who would appreciate it . . . and him.

He turned his smart phone over in his hand and checked his call list. Several high class and very expensive local prostitutes were listed, but they would never understand the significance of what he had achieved. His gaze stopped on a number without a name. He puzzled for a while as to who this number belonged to. Then he remembered . . . Jane, of course! He had copied her number into his phone while she was asleep in the hotel room in London. He realised it was probably she who was responsible for supplying the police file to the CIA and logically if that was true, she must be a CIA agent. That made her a dangerous bedfellow, but Albert craved excitement, and what could be more exciting than inviting the enemy into your exclusive world? He reasoned that whatever she reported back would be of little value to the CIA, plus he could feed her inaccurate data until the CIA suspected her of duplicity and wouldn't know whether to believe her or not. He felt sure she would not try to damage him physically, after all why kill the goose which could potentially lay the golden egg? The CIA must surely have learned that lesson by now. No! They would want him alive and well in order for him to pass on his secrets to them. It would be a two way street, he would be attempting to extract information from her and vice versa. Decision made, he stabbed a finger at the button on his phone.

'Hello?' said a female voice.

'Jane?' said Albert.

'Er . . . yes,' she said, momentarily surprised at the use of one of her aliases.

'This is Albert, remember, from the London hotel?'

There was a faint click on the line as the recorder and tracing system cut in. 'Do you fancy meeting up sometime?' he said.

'Yes! Why not? Are you still in London,' she asked.

Oh she's good, thought Albert. *She must be the only person in Langley who doesn't know where I am. This is going to be fun.* 'No I'm in my penthouse suite in Houston. Why don't you drop in?'

'Sure,' she said, altogether more readily than would be reasonable. 'Let me throw a few things into an overnight bag.'

'I'm on the top floor of the Trust Oil and Gas building. I'll send a cab to meet you at the airport. Will you be arriving from Kennedy?' he said innocently.

'Possibly,' she said thinking quickly, 'it depends on my connections. I'll ring you when I arrive, OK?'

'That's fine, I look forward to seeing you again, bye.'

Albert switched off his phone and smiled to himself, *Now! Who's on which hook?*

Meanwhile in an office at CIA headquarters in Langley, Harry Fowler re-ran the recording and scowled at Jane.

'Have you any idea what this guy is capable of?'

'He won't hurt me Harry,' she smiled, 'he knows I'm CIA, he just wants to play games and it could be useful to have someone on the inside.'

'As far as we know,' insisted Harry, he's responsible for three deaths, possibly four if you count the CEO of the company he's just stolen.'

'But from what your telling me he's killed one of those twice and you're not even sure she's dead yet, so that doesn't count does it?' she said with a mischievous twinkle in her eye.

'Semantics,' growled Harry, 'just be careful.'

. . . .

Jane stepped out of the executive lift on the top floor of the Trust Oil & Gas building and was met by the beaming Albert.

'The last time I saw you, you were employed by Shell, what happened?' she said, checking the plush surroundings approvingly.

'Ja, I did a few deals and here I am.'

He guided her through into the split level lounge, which was dominated by a massive model of the International Space Station, hanging from the ceiling on steel wires.

'Wow!' she said, 'You do like to make a statement don't you?'

'No point in being modest,' he grinned. 'This will be my new headquarters.'

She pointed at the model. 'You mean this?'

He nodded, 'I need to operate from somewhere reasonably safe, where your friends can't reach me.'

She sat down on one of the plush settees and leaned back coquettishly. 'Oh Albert, what an imagination you do have,' she laughed. 'Whatever do you mean . . . "my friends"?'

He leaned over and kissed her lightly on the cheek. 'Come, let me introduce you to your imaginary friends.' He took her by the hand and guided her to the picture window. Jane already knew what she would see there but feigned surprise anyway. 'You seem to be surrounded by snipers, what have you done to deserve so much attention, you naughty boy?'

'It seems I have upset your Mr Philby by not dying at the appropriate time and by exposing the loopholes in his so called national security service. He should really be pleased that I've taken the trouble to help him in this way but he seems to be taking it personally.'

'So what are your plans, how do you propose to make the ISS your headquarters? If you have a rocket somewhere, I wouldn't mind going on that trip with you.'

'And so you shall, but not by rocket.'

'Ah! Let me guess,' she laughed, 'you've found a magic lamp which when rubbed, grants you three wishes.'

'Aha! Now who's being a naughty little spy?' he smiled. 'Slightly more than three!' He sauntered across to the mini bar and poured them drinks. 'What I would like to do is enjoy your company for a few days and then we shall go on our trip. How about you?'

'Sounds great,' said Jane. 'Aren't you afraid I'm going to murder you in your bed?'

'I'm sure the CIA have finally seen sense and realized that I am far more use to them alive than dead, so I expect you've been briefed accordingly.'

'Why are you so sure I'm a CIA agent?'

'That's simple, the British police file could not have been obtained by the CIA in any other way and you were at fourteen Lichfield Crescent asking questions at the same time as me.'

'Quite a coincidence don't you think?' she replied, mischievously.

'It was the classic honey trap wasn't it? And I fell for it. Anyway, quite apart from your instructions, you wouldn't kill me.'

'Oh?' she said.

'You're the sort of person who needs excitement. You wouldn't be here now if you didn't. I expect you were told not to do this; far too dangerous to be liasing with a person like me, but you went ahead with it anyway. I don't flatter myself that you're madly in love with me . . . you're not . . . so it must be for the excitement.'

'So you see us as a modern day "Bonnie and Clyde" getting high on the danger in our relationship?'

'Possibly, of course if you're scared, you can always go back to your boring little desk at Langley and write reports about my exploits.'

'We've done far too much talking already,' she said, downing the contents of her glass. Where's the bedroom, I might want to freshen up . . . or something.'

. . . .

The crew of the International Space Station were gathered together around their communal meal, joking and laughing with each other, pleased with their days work. Matt Goldberg and Igor Chevsky had earlier completed an eight hour, exhausting space walk, correcting minor misalignments in the solar array. This was recurring maintenance work to ensure the array would follow the sun and give maximum power output at all times.

Lindon Johannssen playfully flicked a spoonful of food at Matt and it floated across the intervening space between them delicately coming to rest on his chin. Matt, laughing uproariously, ducked down and skilfully flipped the food into his mouth, then like a dog, begged for more. Suddenly, Lindon looked bemused, 'Where's that spoon gone he exclaimed?' looking around anxiously.

'Must have floated off somewhere,' said Matt.

Lindon, being Finland's first astronaut was quickly nicknamed by the rest of the crew, "Lin the Fin". He pulled a face. 'It felt like it was yanked out of my hand, and then it disappeared.'

Scott Cherney rubbed his nose scornfully. 'You're hallucinating mate, probably space sickness,' he said in a broad Australian accent.

'Well you tell me where it is,' said Lin, rising to the bait, and spreading his hands expectantly.

'Naw, you probably swallowed it mate. With a gob that size you probably didn't even notice.'

Lindon smiled in response. He was well aware of his tendency to talk too much and was quite used to the ribbing. 'I s'pose you keep your spoon in yer tucker bag safe and sound,' he said.

'Too right mate, bonza!'

Matt Goldberg's smile froze on his face as he remembered he had had a similar sensation while shaving that morning, when his razor blade had disappeared, but elected to say nothing. As leader he had no wish to cause unnecessary alarm amongst his crew. More good humoured leg pulling followed until the crew retired to their cubicles for a few hours sleep.

The station's biologist, Lindy Hogan was first to arise, and proceeded to go through the ritual awakening of "ma boys", as she called them, with her Texan drawl. Unusually she found that Lin's cubicle was empty. He was normally the last to arise. Assuming he was taking in one of the many spectacular sunrises, which occurred several times every day, in the cupola chamber, she thought no more of it, until he failed to turn up for breakfast.

'I'm a bit worried about Lin,' she confided to Matt. 'I can't seem to find him anywhere.'

It being Sunday and with a generally reduced workload, Matt enlisted the whole crew to join in the search, but to no avail.

'Well he can't have jumped ship,' said Scott. 'It takes hours to get kitted up, he can't do it on his own; so we can forget "man overboard".'

'You're assuming he wanted to go outside in a suit,' said Chevsky, in his down to earth no nonsense way.

This temporarily brought all conversation to a halt as they considered the terrible prospect that Lin may have deliberately committed suicide in the most horrible way possible, with the blood boiling out of his veins and his body literally exploding into the vacuum outside.

Finally Matt broke the silence. 'For sure if that's what he's done we ain't going to find any sign of him out there. I can't understand it, he was perfectly alright at dinner, he took some stick but that's nothing unusual. Have you checked the CRV and the Soyuz escape vehicles?'

'Yes they're still there,' said Lindy despondently.

Matt plugged in his laptop to a terminal and established communication with the Mission Control Centre in Houston, while the ashen faced crew looked on helplessly.

'Houston we seem to have lost one of our astronauts.' he said.

The Flight Director, Brett Allwood, appeared on the screen. 'Can you repeat that Matt?'

'We've looked everywhere on the ISS but Lin just ain't here anymore.'

There was a prolonged silence from Houston and then Brett came back with, 'Matt, we're going to examine all the possibilities and then come back to you, but at first sight it just doesn't make any sense. The escape vehicles are still in place, so he must be on there somewhere. We'll get back to you.'

'Well, they're just as baffled as we are,' said Matt gloomily, turning his laptop to standby. 'They may know of some man size niches on this rabbit warren that we don't know about.'

Suddenly Lindy had an idea. 'Perhaps he's stuck in one of the airlocks,' she said.

'OK it's worth a look,' said Matt. 'Split up and check all the airlocks.'

The four astronauts went off in different directions . . . but only three came back!

. . . .

Lucy hurried back to Jack's old room, where she found Sophie and Megan chatting like old friends.

'Sophie,' she began, 'I need your help.'

'Yes of course,' she said, beaming at the opportunity to help her new friends, and rising from the bed. Lucy's eyes came to rest on the small scarlet stain on the white sheet where Sophie had been sitting. Sophie's eyes followed hers to the same spot. 'Oh I am so sorry,' she said, 'I intended to ask if you could lend me some . . . ?'

'No problem,' said Megan quickly, 'I'll just go back to my room and get some for you.'

Lucy was caught off balance by the sight of the menstrual blood, her plan being to use Sophie's pregnancy to catch Albert out. Clearly this was no longer possible, and as Sophie had never been aware of her condition she decided to keep it to herself.

Sophie cut across her thoughts. 'What do you want me to do?'

'I have a plan to stop Albert but it will work a lot better if you could help me?'

'You don't intend to kill him do you?' she said.

'No! Much as I would like to. I just want to make it impossible for him to hurt anybody else.'

'So how can I help?'

'I'm not sure yet but for the moment I need to know I can rely on you to help.'

'OK, I'm on your side,' said Sophie resolutely.

'We must transfer your belongings from Amsterdam to here, so I want you to enter the portal with me and concentrate on your home, wherever that is.'

'You want me to live in England?' she said in surprise.

'It's safer that way. If he thinks you're dead, he can't harm you.'

Sophie shot a fearful glance at the portal. 'Does it hurt?'

'Not at all and we shall be going together,' said Lucy, with an encouraging smile.

'OK let's do it, then your young man can have his dressing gown back.'

'Oh! No, Sophie, he's just my best friend. We're not an item,' said Lucy hurriedly.

Lucy thought she detected a glimmer of relief on Sophie's face, but conceded to herself that she may have been mistaken.

. . . .

Sophie's one room flat in the slum area of Amsterdam was a revelation to Lucy. She could not believe that people lived in this sort of squalor and was desperate to get away from there as quickly as possible. For Sophie, it was also a revelation. After she had overcome her initial concerns she seemed to enjoy the experience of being whisked back to her old flat. She packed her few clothes and possessions into a large, cardboard suitcase, excitedly chattering to Lucy the whole time. Once back in Cambridge, she sat on the bed and proudly showed Lucy photographs of her parents in a large scrapbook.

Lucy suddenly pointed at a photograph, 'Who's that?' she cried.

'Ah, yes, that's me and Albert, with Albert's mother.'

'May I borrow it?' said Lucy, excitedly.

'Yes, of course, what are you going to do with it?'

'With your help and this,' Lucy waved the photograph, 'we will bring Albert to justice.'

'I don't understand,' said Sophie with a puzzled frown.

'You will,' said Lucy emphatically, 'you will.'

. . . .

Scott Cherney, Lindy Hogan and Igor Chevsky, were floating in front of the monitor viewing the Houston control room, while a disembodied, reassuring voice was calmly trying to convince them that the problem was soluble.

'S'all right for you mate,' said Scott bitterly. 'You're not whistling round the Earth every ninety minutes, in a tin can, two hundred miles up, with something picking us off one by one.'

'We are just as concerned as you are Scott but at the moment we have no explanation. We're working on it.'

Scott, with a muttered curse, quickly turned away in disgust and bumped into Chevsky causing them both to float over to the other side of the module, in a heap of tangled arms and legs. Lindy concentrated on the screen. She switched the view from the Houston control room to one showing all the ambient data around the space station. Everything appeared to be normal.

'Are there any unusual solar activities in the region, magnetic disturbances, or sun spots? Is there any way we can protect ourselves?' she asked desperately.

'None that we can detect, Lindy,' came the response. 'I think you've just got to stay close together and keep a watch on each other until we come up with something.'

Lindy turned around. 'Here that bo . . . ?'

The words froze on her lips as she realised she was talking to thin air!

· ·

In a New York supermarket a man dressed only in shorts, socks and NASA 'T' shirt was remonstrating with the manager while a group of shoppers looked on in mild amusement.

'Will you please let me use your phone so that I can tell Mission Control, in Houston, where I am?'

'Look sir,' said the manager, rocking backwards and forwards on the balls of his feet, 'if I allowed every crank the use of our phone, there would be a queue outside the door and around the block. Every vagrant for miles around would be in here.'

'Vagrant! How dare you!' shouted Lin, 'I am a NASA astronaut who has just been forcibly removed from the International Space Station by some unknown alien force and dumped in your supermarket.'

The manager examined him with a disdainful glance. 'Well it seems you've got the 'T' shirt, and you're certainly not dressed for the conditions.' He glanced through the glass entrance doors at the large flakes of snow softly descending in the car park outside. 'Where is your car parked sir?'

'I don't have a car.' said Lin, trying to stay calm.

The manager shook his polished, bald head and peered through his half moon spectacles sadly at Lin, now more convinced than ever that this was a drug filled opportunist trying to take advantage of his warm supermarket. 'Have you some form of identification sir?'

'No I do not; all my personal effects are on the Space Station.'

'Yes of course they are sir, I should have realised,' said the manager, waving wildly at a nearby security guard.

The genial man came lumbering over. 'Show this gentleman off the premises would you please Slattery? And help him to find his car,' said the manager haughtily.

Lin made to protest but Slattery gave him a knowing wink, took him by the elbow and steered him towards the exit. When out of earshot of the manager the big man leaned down to Lin's ear. 'Don't mind him none Mr Johannssen, ah recognised you straight away. Ah follow you guys all the time, NASA TV's ma favourite show. All that wizzin' around the Earth, fantastic, ah love it and so too do ma two little boys. They're goin' to be so excited 'cos ah met you.' As they reached the exit Slattery handed him his mobile phone. 'There you go sir, phone Mission Control. This is the most exciting thing in ma life. Ah jus want yer autograph to show ma kids, if yer don' mind sir.'

'Of course, you've saved my life,' said Lin, shivering and gratefully accepting the phone.

Slattery stood by Lin savouring the moment as the astronaut reported his position to the bemused Mission Control Director, in Houston. An hour later Lin was dressed in the finest suit, parka and shoes the supermarket could muster after they had received an outraged phone call from the Mission Control Director promising to advertise their lack of respect for national heroes, albeit Finnish ones. The car park had been cleared to accept the arrival of the NASA helicopter and Slattery had managed to winkle his children out of school to witness the event. The message was quickly flashed up to Lindy Hogan in the space station.

'How did he get there?' she cried, incredulously.

'He doesn't know,' replied Mission Control. 'It's a mystery to everyone, but at least it gives us hope that the rest of the crew will be found.'

'And in the meantime, what do you want me to do?' said Lindy.

'Just sit tight and stay calm, while we try and find the rest of the guys. Then we have to figure out some way of getting them back up there.'

'Yeah! It's kinda lonely up here without the guys,' she said. 'I'm not sure I can keep things ticking over on my own if there's an emergency.'

'Don't worry about it, you won't have to!' boomed a voice at the other end of the Destiny module. 'Ja! Stay calm Lindy, then you will be better able to help your new commander.'

Lindy froze in terror at the sudden arrival of the tall blond man stooping slightly in the limited height of the module. She tried to scream but it would not go past the knot in her throat and resulted instead in a soft strangled cry from which the air had been extracted.

'Who . . . are you?' she managed finally.

'Don't worry Lindy, I mean you no harm, you are far too useful to me. My name is Albert and I am taking over command of this space station. You speak Russian and Chinese?'

'Well . . . er . . . yes, how did you know?'

'Never mind that. Now you are my interpreter,' said Albert, pointing an authoritative finger at her.

She recovered from the shock quickly and enabled Mission Control visual monitoring from all ISS cameras. 'Yes Lindy, are you OK?' queried Houston.

Expecting the intruder to prevent her speaking she gabbled quickly; 'No I'm not! There's a man . . . he just appeared . . . out of nowhere.' She looked around nervously at Albert, who was smiling benignly at her.

'What do you want?' she cried. 'Where did you come from?'

'Lindy?' the voice from Houston interjected, in alarm, 'What's going on?'

Albert, still smiling, floated down the module until he was just behind Lindy's shoulder and could be seen by Mission Control. He looked into the camera. 'I could tell you my ambition is to become a member of the two hundred mile high club. Although I probably wouldn't be the first,' he grinned. 'But there are far more important matters require my attention. Do not worry about Lindy I have another use for her.'

'Who are you? How did you get there?' came the anxious voice of Mission Control.

'My name is Albert Grossman and how I got here is more a matter for your President.'

Suddenly overwhelmed by the situation, Lindy Hogan swam to the far end of the module and began to cry, tears floating from her eyes like tiny colourless balloons.

CHAPTER 20

Rick Newman was standing in the NASA control centre in Washington anxiously watching the monitor screens with Harry Fowler, Alan Philby and the Flight Director, Brett Allwood, who had been rushed up from Houston to help deal with the crisis. Mission Control Houston had patched through the video link to enable the President direct access to the ISS. Several cameras within the Destiny Module were panning around, presenting a comprehensive view of the situation. Suddenly Harry Fowler pointed at one of the monitors and cried, 'Hold that camera!'

'Oh my God!' exclaimed Philby, 'Is that Jane?'

He was referring to what at first looked like a pair of blue NASA dungarees hanging alongside the module wall. On top of this was perched a baseball cap, beneath which could be seen a woman's face. Her chin had sagged to her chest, her cheeks were hollow and there were dark rings under her closed eyes.

'She looks dreadful. She's either been drugged or hypnotised,' said Harry anxiously. 'She thought she could deal with him and now . . . this.'

'Somehow, Harry, we have to get her out of there,' hissed Philby.

'Who is this Grossman fella?' remarked the President incredulously. 'How did he get up there and what's he done with the crew?'

Philby gave a hoarse cough. 'We spoke about him before, Mr President. He's the guy who put an ICBM in Langley.'

'We just don't know how he got there,' said Brett Allwood. 'But we do know what he's done with the astronauts.'

The President looked enquiringly at NASA's director. 'And that is?'

'They're here sir, in a security debrief. Except that is for Lindy Hogan.'

'He transported them back down to Earth?'

'They were sprayed around the country, but we've got all of them back now, yes sir.'

'Why has he kept Lindy?'

The Director spread his hands in a gesture of helplessness. 'Maybe he's kept her as insurance against us cutting off the life support systems.'

'How's he doing this?'

'We have no idea sir.'

The President thought for a moment and popped a jelly bean in his mouth. 'Has he said what he wants?'

'No sir, except that he wants to speak with you,' said Allwood.

'O.K. we have to keep this low key. I need to speak to him and find out what the hell he's after. I want two missiles programmed to destroy the ISS, understood?'

The director nodded uncertainly. The President noted his reluctance and put a reassuring hand on his shoulder. 'Bert,' he murmured 'there are things up there which even you are not aware of. It is better that you do not know what

I know, for if you knew what I know, you wouldn't know what to do about what you don't know.'

Brett was mystified and disturbed; 'How can this be sir? I've lived with this project for over twenty years. There is nothing on that space station which has not first passed by my desk.'

'Trust me Bert, there are things which were not for your approval, to protect you and your family. Things were introduced by previous administrations.'

The mention of his family killed the conversation stone dead. Brett was now in no doubt that whatever it was; he didn't want to know about it.

'Get me connected,' barked the President, 'let's find out what's motivating this lunatic.'

Albert greeted him affably enough. 'Good morning Mr President very kind of you to spare the time sir.'

'Er, good morning,' replied the President. 'Who are you and what do you want?'

'Oh ja! I apologise for not introducing myself. My name is Albert, Albert Grossman, new owner of Trust Oil and Gas. First of all, I feel I have to thank your CIA for presenting me with this wonderful woman,' he indicated the limp figure of Jane. 'She is everything a man could want, completely compliant, and never complains.'

Harry Fowler clenched his fists and growled.

The President stared at the face on the monitor then suddenly recognised him. 'So you're the guy the FBI was trying to pin down after the collapse of Trust Oil and Gas.'

'Yes, that was regrettable. Mr. Adams did not want to do business with me, which I suppose was acceptable, but his insults were not. I sincerely hope that incident would not be repeated with anyone else.'

'So how did you manage to occupy my space station and evict all the crew?'

'First of all Mr President, this is not your space station and secondly I removed the crew for their own safety. After all, I didn't want to be responsible for their deaths if you resort to violence by releasing the two missiles you are currently targeting at the ISS.'

The President was temporarily speechless and looked helplessly at Brett for support. Brett shook his head in mute disbelief.

'How . . . ,' he began, 'what do you want?' he managed to say to Grossman finally.

'I wanted to speak to you on the serious matter of energy, specifically energy derived from oil and then to make you an offer of partnership. Much of the world conflict has been created out of your insatiable thirst for oil. I can eliminate this requirement, but you must accept that I will exclusively control the science I use to achieve this.'

'You offer me something with one hand then take it away with the other?'

'Ja! That is correct. You have already seen what I can do with my new science. At no time did I need oil or any of its by products. Think about that Mr President, you could transport anything anywhere almost instantaneously without the requirement of oil or kowtowing to the oil producing nations. What I am offering you is freedom from the shackles of oil rich dictatorships, complete independence from their petty requirements. I am offering you the opportunity to join an exclusive club which has access to this science but will use it only with permission of the other members, and critically . . . myself.'

'Let me just get this straight, Wilbert. You want me to sign a deal with you that allows you tell me what to do?'

'The name is Albert sir, and the answer is yes.'

'So how's this gonna work?'

'You build the infrastructure and I sell you the franchise to use it, with a clause allowing me to revoke the licence if I, and I alone, believe you are abusing the contract.'

'And what about the military?' said the President.

'Same deal,' said Albert, emphatically.

'You want me to hand over control of this great country's military prowess to you?' snapped the astonished President.

'I already control it,' said Albert. 'I would just be selling it back to you . . . on lease.'

The President turned to Brett and made a circular motion with his finger against his temple. 'Mr Grossman,' he said, 'I cannot conduct negotiations like this; I believe this should be done face to face.'

The NASA director tapped him on the shoulder. 'Missiles are ready sir,' he mouthed.

The President covered the microphone with one hand. 'Blow the bastard out of the sky,' he whispered.

Brett made to object. 'But Mr President, we can't just blow it up, what about Lindy . . . the Japanese . . . the Russians, all those years of scientific experiment . . . ?'

The President paused for a moment then popped a jelly bean in his mouth and offered one to Brett from his crumpled paper bag. Brett stared at the bag in horror and declined the offer then at the President's face which was set in a determined grimace.

'Do it!' he growled, 'It was an accident, happens all the time with the space programme. It's a high risk business; all we have to do is cover it up. I can't afford to have this idiot dictating to me in an election year, do you understand?'

Brett nodded dumbly and scurried away to give the order to the missile launch crew.

'I agree with your suggestion, Mr President, we should have face to face negotiations,' interrupted Albert.

The President smiled knowingly, covered the telephone microphone once more with his hand and addressed Harry Fowler. 'Get ready to terminate the bastard if he's stupid enough to show up,' he said cheerfully. 'We'll nail him either way.'

Alan Philby cut in frantically, 'We can't do that sir he's rigged all our ICBM's to explode in their silos if we kill him.'

There was a short pause and Albert disappeared off the screen.

'He's bluffing Ira, nobody can do that without my permission. I've got the codes!' He waved a dismissive hand at the objection. 'Ready!' cried the President expectantly.

'But sir you don't understand!' The panic stricken Philby, addressed the empty space where the President had been standing.

The President suddenly re-appeared beside Albert on the space station!

'Oh dear,' said Albert mockingly, 'what have I done? Did I mishear? Did you say that two of your missiles are streaking towards us as we speak? It seems we must negotiate fairly rapidly Mr. President, I estimate three minutes at most,' he said, looking at his watch with a knowing smile.

CHAPTER 21

The lunchtime rush in the canteen had abated and Dipper had gone in search of second helpings, leaving his mobile phone on the table. Chu sat sipping his tea reflectively, wondering how Lucy was doing, when the phone rang. He looked around but there was no sign of Dipper. Picking it up, he pressed the accept button and said, 'Hello!'

There followed a brief silence and then a male voice said, 'is that Dipper?'

'No this is Chu,' said the Chinaman.

Chu thought he detected a sharp intake of breath at the other end of the phone, then the line went dead. Dipper returned with a plateful of leftovers and sat down heavily.

Chu eyed him critically. 'You eating too much,' he said.

'Possibly,' Dipper agreed, 'but I have to feed the grey matter.'

'It not your brain that concern me,' said Chu glancing at the ever expanding girth. 'Anyway, you have phone call, but rang off without explaining.'

Dipper picked up his mobile and stabbed at a few buttons. 'Don't recognise the number,' he said, pressing call.

The line emitted tele-printer chattering noises but nothing else. He passed the phone to Chu who listened intently to the noise.

'Encryption!' he stated knowledgeably.

Dipper placed the phone back in his pocket with a puzzled frown. 'Well, whoever it was didn't want me to ring back,' he said and tucked into his supplementary dinner.

· ·

Chu was enjoying himself later that afternoon, lecturing a class of bright young students, who were bombarding him with questions on the subject of the "Higgs Boson", the particle credited with investing all other particles with their mass, when a black helicopter landed on the grass outside the window. Welcoming the brief respite he joined the rest of the students at the window as they peered out at the unmarked machine. Three men dressed in balaclavas and black overalls tumbled out of the machine and headed directly for the physics faculty. Chu began to feel uneasy when he spotted the rifles tucked under their arms. He made an excuse to his students, saying he was going to the toilet. He didn't get that far. The men in black had obviously done their homework and arrested him before he set foot in the toilet block. His students watched in amazement as he was bundled into the helicopter. With a loud roar of the rotor blades, it took off and headed south. Dipper watched in anguish as his mentor was whisked away. Then he remembered the phone call Chu had answered earlier. 'That was more than a coincidence,' he muttered, 'he's been kidnapped.' The whole thing was over in less than two minutes and was conducted with military efficiency, reinforcing Dipper's belief he had been arrested by the S.A.S.

'But why?' he asked himself. 'Something big is underway.'

His curiosity thoroughly aroused, he scurried back to his room and switched on Lucy's laptop, then loaded the programme DVD. His progress was immediately halted by the password requirement, which he knew he would never be able to guess. He was sitting despondently, gazing at the screen when a tinny little voice said, 'you want some herp Dipper?' The jolt of being confronted by Crip sent a shock wave from the top of his head through his flabby body, leaving him trembling like a jelly.

'Who . . . ? what . . . ? what are you?' he stammered.

'I Crip,' he said with a flourish, 'and this Dunnit.'

Dunnit appeared and puffing out his chest, smiled up at Dipper.

Dipper mopped the cold sweat off his brow with an unwholesome handkerchief, turned around and looked out of the window while he counted to ten. When he turned back, they were still there, looking bemused by his actions.

'Don't upset yourself, old boy,' said Dunnit with a smile, 'we're here to help you. Now, how can we be of assistance?'

With a tremendous effort, Dipper ignored the bizarre nature of the conversation he was having and asked; 'Do you know where Chu's been taken?'

'No, but my helpful friend and I will certainly find out young sir, and let you know forthwith. Take heart, we shall find him,' and they both vanished.

Dipper was startled once more as a short time later they re-appeared, both beaming broadly. 'We find, we find,' said Crip. 'He in London, at Ten Downing Street.'

'But that's the Prime Minister's address,' said Dipper.

'Oh! Is it? We no know that,' said Crip.

'Of course we do,' interjected Dunnit. 'I told you it was earlier.'

'No you didn't, you make me look like fool.'

'Crip! You don't need me to make you look like a fool.'

'Er . . . boys,' interrupted Dipper, 'do you know what Chu's doing there?'

'Oh yes,' said Dunnit, 'he's been interviewed by MI6. They're asking him questions about the programme, but he won't tell them anything.'

Suddenly Dipper had an idea. 'Is there any way you can transmit what's happening to this screen?' he said, pointing at the laptop.

'Oh, we no allowed to do that,' said Crip, doubtfully. 'We no programmed for that.'

'Hold on a minute old chap,' said Dunnit. 'You're forgetting we've been evolving and can do things now which we're not supposed to do.'

'Ah so!' exclaimed Crip excitedly. 'You right, we strike blow for emancipation of computer generated icons,' he shouted, raising a clenched fist . . . 'let's try.'

With that they both disappeared and the screen went blank. A little while later, Dipper was enjoying himself enormously as he watched Chu boxing shadows with the MI6 officer in a Downing Street ante room. MI6 had clearly not been briefed and were not aware of the reason for the abduction. Chu was playing the wronged innocent brilliantly. The phone rang and after a short conversation they were joined by a technician who set up a teleconference video link to Washington and the Deputy Director of the CIA, Alan Philby.

'Good afternoon Mr Chu, we have been trying to have a conversation with you for some time, but we understood you to be in China. Why have you now appeared in England?'

'Hello Mr Philby preased to meet with you . . . yes, Chinese police want to kill me. I had to leave.'

'Do you have a passport Mr Chu?'

'No sir, had to leave quickly without it.'

'How did you get into England?'

'I use programme to teleport myself.'

'Would you be willing to give us your programme?'

Dipper could see Chu stiffen. 'No! I not give secret to anyone.'

Unfazed, Philby continued the conversation. 'If you are not prepared to share your knowledge with anyone, can you explain how Albert Grossman came by it?'

'He stole from my daughter.'

'And then killed her and your ex wife?'

'Yes sir.'

'So I assume you would want to bring Grossman to justice?'

'Yes sir.'

'Mr Chu, I have to tell you that we believe you are the only person who can help us to do this.'

'Oh?'

'You see, Mr Grossman has taken over the International Space Station and we are powerless to do anything about it. Only you can help us.'

'Why does he do this?'

'His motives are difficult to understand, but we believe he wants to retain total control of your programme for his own ends.'

'I see,' said Chu. 'So what . . . ah . . . you expect me to do?'

'We're not sure what you can do but you seem to be the only person who can do anything at all?'

'So, I not under arrest?'

'No Mr Chu.'

'Then I free to go?' he said rising from his chair.

'Well there is a little matter of illegal entry to the country,' said Philby. 'I'll leave our friends from MI6 to deal with you on that score. They may wish to return you to China . . . and your uncertain future.'

Chu sat down again. 'He very dangerous man, already killed my family, he not hesitate to kill me as well.'

'Yes we understand that. We must work something out which will protect you at the same time. First of all would you be willing to transport yourself to Mission Control in Houston?'

'If choice is China and death, or Houston with chance of life, then answer is . . . ah . . . obvious,' said Chu with a wry smile, pulling his smart phone from his pocket.

The MI6 officer watched with professional interest as Chu hunted around a pocket in his voluminous trousers, finally pulling out a memory chip.

'Have not had time to fit or test yet,' he said apologetically fitting the chip in his phone.

He pressed buttons on his phone with no obvious result, and the MI6 officer began to fidget. Then he vanished! 'Whoops!' said Chu, making for the door. Before he reached it, he too disappeared, leaving Philby talking to an empty room. Chu made contact with the disorientated officer in his state of pure energy, erased his memory of the interview, and then returned him to the material world.

Dipper applauded excitedly as Chu appeared in his room. 'Crip set up a remote viewer so I was watching your interview with the CIA,' he said. 'It was brilliant! What's happening in the ISS? Who's this Albert Grossman? Why are you involved?'

Chu held up his hands defensively. 'You have so many questions young man. Prease to be patient and I will explain soon. I must attend to other matters first. You say Crip did this?' Chu, indicated the laptop, which was still showing the interview room, a very confused MI6 officer and the irate Philby on the video link.

'Yes.'

'But he not programmed to do this.'

'Well he did mention something about evolving and striking a blow for the emancipation of computer generated icons,' chuckled Dipper.

The wrinkles around Chu's eyes creased in delight. 'He very mischievous, must punish him severely,' he said, calling up the help screen. The screen appeared showing Crip lying in bed, looking very sorry for himself, his eyes bleary and his nose bright red. Dunnit appeared carrying a tray on which sat a mysterious brown bottle labelled "AV".

'What happened?' said Chu, in surprise.

Crip sniffed miserably. 'Me not well.'

'Terribly sorry Mr Chu,' said Dunnit, 'but we appear to be indisposed, cut down, as you might say, with a virus designed to prevent us from working.'

'Grossman did this?'

'I'm afraid Mr Grossman finally found a way to stop us opposing him,' said Dunnit, blowing his nose vigorously.

'OK!' grinned Chu, 'I have answer for you. Doctor Dipper here can devise anti virus programme while I attend to other matters.'

Dipper beamed with excitement at this sudden elevation of his status. 'What are you going to do now?' he said.

'Need to see . . . ah . . . what happening on ISS,' said Chu.

CHAPTER 22

———————————•●•———————————

The President's feet lifted from the floor, his body tumbled over helplessly and he was violently sick, causing a major problem within the confined space. Lindy quickly sprang into action with a hand held vacuum cleaner and managed to clear the module of most of the debris. He began to cough, each convulsion causing him to be projected helplessly backwards. Finally he located a hand hold on the wall and hung there gasping for breath in the alien atmosphere of the International Space Station.

'I would remind you, Mr President, you have only three minutes left before you die at your own hand. You may wish to do something about that . . . write a will perhaps,' grinned Albert evilly.

'What do you mean?' shouted Lindy.

'He's ordered the Space Station to be destroyed,' said Albert calmly. 'Don't worry Lindy you and I will not be on it if he succeeds. I shall take you with me.'

'Take me where?' she screamed in alarm.

'I will take you away from the knee jerk, destructive tendencies, of your incompetent leader.'

The President's face contorted in horror as he realised where he was and what he had done. 'Lindy!' he yelled, 'How do I . . . ?'

'. . . get in touch with Mission Control?' she finished.

She pressed a keystroke button on an adjacent laptop and pushed him in front of the screen. 'Stop them!' he screamed.

Brett's face appeared on the screen. 'Mr President!' he said in astonishment, 'How did you get there?'

'Never mind that now Brett, stop those bloody missiles!'

'Too late I'm afraid sir, they're passed self destruct and I can do nothing with them.'

The President whipped round desperately looking to Albert for help, but he was no longer there.

. . . .

After a few minutes Albert appeared once more in the Destiny Module. The President watched him anxiously, 'What's happening?' he whispered hoarsely, beads of cold sweat floating from his forehead.

Albert shook his head disapprovingly. 'Ja! What a total waste of money. You are a political cowboy, aren't you Mr President?'

The President looked puzzled and a little hurt, nobody had ever spoken to him like this before and he felt he should be resenting it. The circumstances however dictated a certain amount of humility if he wished to survive the ordeal.

'I have diverted your missiles and they are now heading for the sun,' Albert continued with a scathing look. He switched off all Houston's cameras and communication systems. 'So, now we must get down to business. I have produced here a draft treaty for your signature.'

'A treaty?' repeated the relieved and puzzled President.

'Yes a set of rules if you like, which will allow me to decide if you can use my technology or not.'

'You are dictating to me . . . the President of the United States of America, what I can and can't do?'

Albert's manner changed abruptly. 'Cut the crap! You're in no position to get arrogant. Do you realise how cold it is outside?' He whacked the module wall with his fist for emphasis, causing the President to jump nervously. 'That would freeze your prospects for the upcoming election,' he added.

Lindy floated across the module towards them looking apprehensive. 'Mr President,' she said respectfully, 'I think you should listen to what he has to say at least, then decide if you should go along with it or not.'

The President was now gaining confidence as he became more familiar with his surroundings He had recovered from his space sickness, and the threat of extinction by his own hand had receded. The condescending Hollywood smile returned. 'Thank you Lindy, for cleaning up the mess, but I think you should leave this to me.'

Suitably chastened, Lindy retired to the opposite end of the module and busied herself attempting to revive the apparently lifeless Jane.

Albert looked at the President quizzically. 'You just don't get it yet do you?' he said, 'What I am offering you is technology which will transform the way America and the whole world, for that matter, functions. It would release you from your dependence on oil for transport, if you accept my terms and conditions.'

'And what are these "terms and conditions"?' said the President with a sarcastic grimace.

Albert handed him a single sheet of paper, neatly typed with a space for four signatures at the bottom.

'I can't read this,' he said and tried to throw it on the floor. The paper floated out of his hand then swept upwards and clamped itself on his face.

'How undignified,' chuckled Albert, and retrieved it with a flourish. 'Why can't you read it? I hadn't realised you'd added illiteracy to your list of talents.'

'Because I don't have my reading glasses,' he cried triumphantly.

Albert handed the paper to Lindy. 'Read it for Mr President,' he said.

Lindy scanned the paper quickly and glanced at Albert questioningly. 'But this is written in Chinese and Russian as well as English,' she said.

'Just read the English version please.'

'I the undersigned,' she began, 'do hereby relinquish all claims to the programme hereafter referred to as "Grossman Transport Services" or "GTS" for short. I will abide by any decision of Albert Grossman regarding the limits of release of any services to my government as he, and he alone, should see fit. I agree that ultimate control and subsequent development of GTS will be the sole responsibility of Albert Grossman and will only be available under his strict jurisdiction. Financial arrangements are to be negotiated and decided in due course. Should Albert Grossman wish to retract services previously granted, the recipient of these services will repatriate to the owner, Albert Grossman, all aspects of the programme previously granted, without exception.'

'Humph!' muttered Newman, 'And if I don't sign it?'

'You will be the first American President to go down in history, who deliberately disadvantaged his country in order to preserve his over inflated ego.'

'We can only be disadvantaged if some other country's advantaged. You're not suggesting that tin pot, little back street country of yours will be better off than us, are you?' With this he roughly yanked his bag of jelly beans out of his pocket. The contents floated into the far reaches of the module.

'Not at all Mr President, I wouldn't presume to try and upstage your magnificent country, but others would. Lindy, would you please release the air lock door for me?'

'All very well,' grunted the President, perceiving the obvious flaw, 'what do we do when you die?'

'I have no intention of dying,' replied Albert. 'My quest for a new world order requires me to be immortal, and this is readily achieved as a by product of this technology.'

The President's jaw dropped. 'Are you telling me you can have eternal life?'

'I can reinstall my consciousness into new bodies, or reconstitute this one, indefinitely, which I suppose, is the same thing.'

Suddenly perceiving possible personal advantage, the President became much more amenable to negotiation. 'Anyone can do this?'

'Yes, but I would only grant this for the good of society as a whole. You would have to earn it through your services to mankind. I would be the final arbiter, as stated in the agreement.' Albert jabbed an aggressive finger at the document, still held by Lindy.

'So that's the carrot, what's the stick?'

'I'll come to that presently. First of all let me introduce you to the other people who may be advantaged by your reluctance, and at your cost.' Lindy swung back the airlock door and the horizontal, unconscious forms of the Russian President and Chinese Premier floated into the module!

. . . .

The President gaped in astonishment and made a grab at a passing jelly bean. 'How the hell do you do this?' he exclaimed.

'It seems like a common problem across continents that world leaders mislay their shaving kit, just long enough for me to extract some DNA,' smirked Albert.

He floated the two leaders into the centre of the module and parked them side by side. 'Now, if I don't get three signatures on this piece of paper, none of you get anything,' he said. When I wake these two, it's in your interest to encourage them to sign up for the deal, understood?'

The consummate politician, with his eyes firmly fixed on eternal life, nodded dumbly. Albert had a convert!

Pandemonium ensued in the module when Albert injected the two leaders with his "wake up" drug and Lindy was kept busy trying to pacify them in their respective languages for some time. They finally calmed down when they realised there was nowhere for them to go and they were entirely dependent on Albert for their continued well being. At first they assumed they had been kidnapped by the American government and held as hostages. With a few simple party tricks Albert was able to convince them that he was the person they had to deal with and not Rick Newman. Lindy seemed a little overawed by the august assembly of world leaders but Albert waved aside her doubts saying, 'They're only people like you, who just happen to be in charge of their countries . . . at the moment.' He introduced her as his translator and addressed the three leaders, allowing time between statements for Lindy to translate.

'Gentlemen,' he began, 'I apologise for the manner in which I have brought you together. There are two reasons for this; one, it eliminates all your so called advisors and their hidden agendas, and two, demonstrates the power of the computer science I have at my exclusive command. I can totally transform the way goods and people are transported around the world and beyond. As you have already witnessed this does not require any type of fuel whatsoever but is accomplished by the means of converting matter to pure energy and information. The only use for oil after this technology has been introduced world wide, would be for heating and power generation. This would eliminate a major source of conflict between you gentlemen, particularly in the Middle East. I am prepared to offer you this remarkable facility . . . at a price.' All three nodded their agreement. *So far so good,* thought Albert, *they understood "price"*. 'However,' he continued, 'the potential for waging war will be increased dramatically. Your weapons could be transferred anywhere around the globe in an instant, virtually undetected. For this reason I decided the technology cannot be made available to you unless you are prepared to use it responsibly.'

As Lindy translated this into Russian, the Russian President's face became beetroot coloured and he began shouting abuse at Albert. The Chinese Premier watched with his arms folded in mild amusement, as though this outburst was not unexpected. Albert waited patiently for the anger to subside, then continued, 'I have drawn up a treaty which I insist must be signed by all three of you before I consider allowing you access to this facility.'

At this the Russian President began yelling once more and swam towards the module exit.

'What's he saying?' Albert asked Lindy.

'He's refusing to co-operate, let alone sign your treaty,' she said.

'OK let him stew, he'll come back when he's hungry,' said Albert.

Sure enough after half an hour of sulking he realised that he may be being excluded from something advantageous to himself and swam back into the module. He regained his place in a semi circle in front of the laptop giving a live picture of the Earth below their feet. The Space Station was just crossing the Chinese coastline and Albert adjusted the zoom to show the Lodi desert, an area previously used by China for the testing of nuclear weapons.

'Now for the stick,' he said to the American President. 'Just in case you are in doubt as to my ability to enforce the treaty I have arranged a little demonstration.' The three men craned forward expectantly surveying the screen. He turned to the Russian President, 'I have previously transported one of your nuclear warheads into the Lop Nur desert and I will now cause it to explode.'

As Lindy translated, murmurings of discontent came from the three men. Suddenly Albert clicked his fingers and the pressure wall was evident from the blast of the nuclear explosion. The characteristic mushroom cloud then followed while the three men hung in absolute silence, mesmerised by the unfolding drama taking place two hundred miles below. Suddenly they erupted in noisy outrage, Lindy translated the Chinese Premier's comment as, 'You cannot do this in our territory!'

Albert spread his hands. 'So stop me,' he said invitingly.

The Russian President, an expert in martial arts, lunged at his throat. Albert gritted his teeth and disappeared. His attacker sailed on and head butted a metal obstruction fixed to the wall of the module. Bleeding from the head wound, he slowly rolled over onto his back, unconscious. Lindy broke open a first aid kit and went over to attend to him. The remaining two leaders, stunned by what had just happened looked at each other apprehensively. Albert suddenly re-appeared at the far end of the module laughing uproariously.

'Sign the treaty,' he grinned, 'if you wish to be part of the future, but . . . I *will* retain total control.'

The Russian President regained consciousness and the unfortunate Lindy had the task of mopping up last night's vodka, as he heaved uncontrollably.

CHAPTER 23

Once more the three leaders grouped around Albert, arguing noisily as best they could in their different languages. Albert produced copies of the agreement and handed them out to the Chinese leader and the Russian President. For a short while there was silence as they digested his demands.

'Niet!' shouted the Russian, 'Niet!'

'Ja!' said Albert, 'You don't have to join the club, but you will be disadvantaged if the others do.'

'Niet!' He screamed, as Lindy translated.

Albert turned to the screen showing their passage above the Earth once more. 'Further to that little demonstration, I have placed nuclear devices in the Kremlin, the White House, and the People's Congress building in Tiannaman Square.'

Lindy translated with a trembling voice. The Russian President rose up to the same height as Albert and pressed his forehead against Albert's nose. With a sharp movement of his head he attempted a blow made ineffectual by the lack of gravity. 'Niet! Niet! Niet!' He screamed. Albert flushed in anger and clicked his finger at the screen. All watched in horror as the familiar mushroom shaped cloud enveloped Moscow on the ground below. The Russian leader's eyes bulged in fright as he saw what Albert had done. He slumped in a heap on the floor and began crying uncontrollably while the other two leaders hung silent, in the air, like two damp rags on a washing line.

'So!' said Albert, 'Now do we have an agreement?'

The monitor screen flickered and the picture of Moscow, obscured by a nuclear explosion, disappeared. It was replaced by the face of an attractive blond woman. Albert stared in shock and surprise. 'Sophie?' he gasped.

'Yes it's me Albert. The one you cruelly destroyed as your father did to your mother. You left me, a helpless mess of body parts and then forgot about the dreadful thing you had done. You abandoned me after all we've been through together, everything we meant to each other, through all the bad times, remember Albert? All your words of love meant nothing, and then you left me to die!'

Albert was too stunned to speak, then finally he stammered; 'I . . . I . . . I am so sorry Sophie, it was an accident, I didn't mean to . . .'

'Please don't cause any more suffering,' she interrupted. 'I beg you, give this up now then perhaps we can move back into your flat together.'

Albert's mind was in turmoil. 'But I've come so far . . . ,' he said. 'There's so much more . . . we . . . yes, we could do together. Look what I have done already . . . we will be rich, I must carry on.'

The face on the screen faded and was replaced with that of a much older woman, her voice becoming deeper. Albert propelled himself towards the apparition, his eyes wild and staring. 'Mama!' he shouted, 'We have our revenge. Jon Grossman is dead, beaten to death by my hand. I did this for you Mama!'

He was so engrossed and shocked that he didn't notice his pocket being picked and the chip in his smart phone being substituted. From her position of invisible observer, Lucy smiled to herself. Sophie had played her part to perfection. All she had to do now was implement the second part of the plan.

Suddenly, the Russian President felt a cold metallic object in the palm of his hand. A gun! His reaction was instinctive and immediate, retribution for the destruction of Moscow uppermost in his mind. Quickly cocking the weapon he aimed it deliberately at Albert's head. Rick Newman, seeing this, knocked the gun aside. 'Don't!' he screamed, 'This guy can make us immortal; if you kill him he'll blow up the USA!' Ignoring the interruption, the Russian took deliberate aim and pulled the trigger. A small flag appeared at the end of the muzzle, with the word "Bang!" written on it. Out of the corner of his eye Albert saw the gun, instinctively gritted his teeth and disappeared. The Russian swore and waved the pistol aggressively at the space where Albert had been.

'I'll take that if I may,' said a young girl's voice behind him. Lucy held out her hand. 'There aren't any bullets in it. After all you might have hurt somebody.'

The three men swung around to greet this unlikely intruder. The American President was the first one to speak, 'Who the hell are you?' he shouted.

'Lucy Chu, at your service,' she replied. 'My father and I invented the programme stolen by Albert Grossman.'

Albert, in his dematerialised state, sensed that all was not well with the programme in his smart phone. Already disorientated, he panicked, fearing he may not be able to return to three dimensions. He hastily attempted to materialise. Lindy and the three leaders gave a gasp of astonishment at the thing which suddenly appeared and hung in mid air, legs and tail flailing uselessly.

Lucy moved forward and pointed at the object explaining first in English, then in Chinese; 'This is a fine example of a giant salamander, a species of lizard indigenous to China. It can grow to six foot long. The salamander is a particularly good subject for scientific regenerative process study, as it has the ability to re-grow limbs which have been lost. This feature of its DNA attracted our attention when investigating the possibility of transporting human beings using their DNA, computer programmes and quantum entanglement. Unfortunately, this particular one has a serious problem.' She whacked it on the back and it spun around violently, coughed and spat something out of its mouth. Lucy trapped the ejected wireless switch between finger and thumb, interrupting its progress across the module and showed it to her astonished audience. 'This one,' she continued, 'is only part lizard; the other part is what passes for a human being.' She turned the beast around and pointed to its eyes. 'These are not the eyes of a salamander, nor are salamanders normally pink!' Fascinated, her audience peered closely at the eyes, which were undeniably human and obviously terrified. 'The reason this giant salamander has blue eyes, eyelids and pink skin, is because it is part salamander and part Albert Grossman. What a dreadful fate, you may say . . . but, believe me, it is entirely deserved.' She stared deliberately at the eyes. The beast blinked and took on a pleading appearance. 'I said you would regret that slap,' she whispered. She turned her back on the creature and once more addressed her enraptured audience.

She would never have imagined in her wildest dreams that this group of the world's most powerful men would one day be hanging on her every word in this way. With Lindy, now enthusiastically supplying translation, Lucy continued with her speech.

'What you have seen today is spectacular science put to spectacularly bad use. You have witnessed the results and I leave you to form your own conclusions about your own part in this debacle. In some ways Grossman was right. You are too immature to deal with this science and it does require firm control, which he believed could not be implemented by yourselves. I therefore ask that my father and I should be left in peace to pursue our studies without fear of political interference. When the time is right and you are all agreed, we can, in a spirit of harmony, implement the fantastic advantages this science will bring to the human race without creating enmity between you. Also, please remember that whatever Grossman could do . . . so could we. You would never be able to hold us long enough to get the secret of this science without our permission!'

Suddenly Chu appeared in the module smiling and clapping. 'Well done my daughter,' he cried as he floated to greet her. He hugged her to him, gently stroking her hair. 'So you turned him into giant salamander? How very . . . ah . . . "Kafkesque". I didn't know you could be so cruel.'

'It was appropriate Father. He killed my mother. He will now have some fifty years, the average lifespan of a salamander, to reflect on his misdeeds. A human consciousness trapped in the body of a lizard.'

'Ah yes!' said Chu, 'We must speak about this later.'

The Chinese Premier became agitated as he recognised the new intruder. Lindy translated his comments for the benefit of the US President. 'He says this man was arrested recently for committing crimes against the state, and then escaped.'

Chu swam across to his leader and they began a prolonged conversation, occasionally involving Lucy. Finally the Premier beamed at Chu and embraced both of them. The Russian President glowered and spoke to Lindy. 'He's very upset about the holocaust in Moscow,' she said.

'As would I be, if it were true,' said Lucy, overhearing their conversation and smiling.

She motioned them to gather around the monitor screen once more and brought up the picture of the mushroom cloud hanging over Moscow. With a deft flick of her finger she rubbed out the nuclear explosion revealing the untouched city below. 'Full of little tricks was Albert,' she said brightly, 'including "Photoshop".'

The Russian President, overjoyed at this revelation, grabbed Lucy by the waist and crushed her to him. 'Spasiba! Spasiba!' he shouted and kissed her on both cheeks.

Lucy wriggled free from his bear like grip and swam to the side of the module to get her breath back.

Rick Newman was peeved. 'Hell! This Grossman guy was going to make us immortal and now you've turned him into a lizard. You should at least keep that promise.'

With a great effort of will, Lucy addressed the American President in a restrained manner. 'Grossman made no such promise and neither will I.'

Newman made to protest but seeing the determination on Lucy's face decided to save that argument for another day. 'How do we know that you won't hold us to ransom same as this Grossman guy?' he said, pointing at Chu and indicating the other two leaders with a wave of his other hand.

'How do I know, if I give secret to you, you use for the benefit of all mankind?' responded Chu, with an amused twinkle in his eye. 'You will gain nothing from pursuing us except delay in our acceptance of you as responsible recipients. Only when you prove worth,' he indicated all three leaders, 'would we release this science. You understand?'

After Lindy's translation all three nodded.

'I want no piece of signed paper,' said Chu. 'This is matter of honour. Honour very important in China and you must respect this.'

The Russian President waved his clenched fists. 'We must reward Lucy Chu for rescuing us from this tyrant,' he shouted. Lindy translated and Rick Newman applauded reluctantly, while the Chinese Premier showed his enthusiastic approval by bowing and nodding furiously.

CHAPTER 24

———•❖•———

Lucy and Chu accompanied the President into the oval office and sat down on the settee in front of his desk. Lucy felt distinctly underdressed in her shabby jumper, cut off jeans, and trainers but nobody seemed to mind very much. The President excused himself, saying he would return shortly and they were enthusiastically served tea by the First Lady. 'You must be hungry,' she said. 'Can I organise some food for you?'

Lucy nodded vigorously. 'Hamburger with fries,' she said as her stomach rumbled in response.

It had taken Lucy and Chu several hours to return the Chinese and Russian leaders to their countries and transfer the astronauts back to the space station. Jane had been taken directly to hospital for emergency treatment, believed to be suffering from a drugs overdose. This operation was watched with some interest by a strange looking individual dressed in a slightly shabby, faded, sports coat and wearing a bow tie, whom the President introduced as Jeremy. He was now perched awkwardly on a hard back chair, staring straight ahead. Lucy leaned over to Chu and nodded in Jeremy's direction. 'Autistic,' she whispered. Chu admonished her with a look which had little effect. He recognised the symptoms. Lucy was bored. He knew from past experience that this was normally when she became mischievous and felt himself becoming tense as a result. The First Lady tried desperately to break the ice in her best hostess manner but Lucy was having none of it. Dreading what might happen, Chu attempted to involve Jeremy in conversation.

'You work in White House?' he said.

Jeremy inclined his head slightly and continued to gaze at the far wall. 'No I work at Langley, CIA headquarters,' he replied.

'What you do there?' asked Chu politely.

Before Jeremy could reply the door swung open and the President walked in followed by Alan Philby and Harry Fowler. He offered everyone a jelly bean, popped one in his mouth then sat behind his desk.

'I need hardly remind you,' he said, addressing the CIA contingent, 'that this is an election year and every effort must be made to maximise my standing in the eyes of the electorate.'

Harry Fowler, the least political person in the CIA group, suppressed a yawn, *another speech*, he thought.

As if suddenly realising the real purpose of the meeting, the President smiled and turned to Lucy and Chu. 'I owe you both an immense debt of gratitude. I realise you must be exhausted by your efforts but I just had to get you folks together with my operatives to thank you personally for all you've done and to offer you a job with us.'

Lucy felt something akin to an electric shock shake her body and employed her meditation skills to stifle the bellicose response which was on the tip of her tongue. Chu, sensing her discomfort jumped in quickly.

'That very kind of you Mr President, but understand we are scientists. Money and status not concern us and we will not have loyalty to it, as explained before on ISS.'

Harry Fowler grinned to himself. *Oh boy; this could get interesting after all.*

Unperturbed, the President continued with, 'This here is Jeremy, he works on much the same sort of thing as you folks do and he would like to assist you where possible.'

'I'm sure he would,' whispered Lucy to herself.

Fortunately the hamburger and fries arrived at this juncture and Lucy's mood lifted immediately as she tucked in with gusto, while the rest of the group looked on enviously.

Jeremy, taking his cue from the President ignored Lucy completely and addressed Chu; 'For some time my department in the CIA have been investigating the phenomenon which you appear to have mastered,' he said. 'Of course the theory of quantum entanglement is well known to us but the practical application was always thought to be impossible, mainly because of the massive amount of computing power required. It would seem you have overcome this problem to such a degree that you can teleport people with as little memory as exists in a smart phone.'

Chu nodded his agreement.

'Obviously we are curious to understand how you do this,' said Jeremy expectantly.

Chu remained silent, while Lucy continued to concentrate on her burger. The President chipped in to bridge the embarrassing gap in the conversation.

'Why, if we had this technology we could put men on Mars by the beginning of the new year and save billions of dollars into the bargain. Imagine that! And in an election year! You would be rich young lady, I would see to that personally,' he said pointing at Lucy, perceiving her to be the most likely out of the two to jump at financial inducements.

'Mr President,' she said through a mouthful of burger, 'if I wanted to be rich, I could be without your help. Understand that I can turn any metal into gold, if I desired it.'

'You can?' gasped the President his eyes wide with astonishment and sudden interest.

'Certainly,' she said emphatically.

'In large quantities?'

'Yes,' Lucy chuckled.

'Well, imagine that,' he said, clapping his hands together excitedly. 'Gentlemen we've got ourselves a little gold mine here.'

'Contain your excitement, Mr President, I've no intention of becoming your pet goose laying golden eggs,' said Lucy testily.

Rick Newman's frustration began to overcome any diplomacy. 'What do you folks want? State yer price!' he cried.

'Let me remind you Mr. President, of our conversation while on ISS. We will not give this information to anyone we consider to be inappropriate,' cut in Chu.

'And you think that I'm . . . inappropriate?'

'Regrettably, yes,' said Chu.

Alan Philby shuffled uncomfortably and coughed, seeking to come to his President's assistance. 'You do realise,' he said quickly, 'the Russians and Chinese will make your life intolerable. They'll pursue you until you give in. We can offer you protection from all that, if you come and work here.'

'And you make . . . ah . . . our lives no less intolerable,' said Chu, smiling benignly, 'by turning our science into a weapon of war, in pursuit of world domination. This is unacceptable.'

Alan Philby weighed in once more. 'This will happen anyway when the Chinese, Russians or ourselves discover the secret without your help.'

'Then it will not be by my hand and I have no responsibility for result,' smiled Chu.

'There are two other members of your group,' said Philby, trying to build pressure on Chu.

Finally all Lucy's efforts at polite conversation failed. 'You'll get the same response from them,' she snapped. 'As you have already seen, you can't hold them for interrogation, if that's what you had in mind. Have you brought us here to simply offer inducements, or threats? Either way it's morally repugnant. And as a woman I resent your wizened pet academic talking through me as if I didn't exist. Be aware that this sort of treatment automatically reduces the possibility of us ever . . . ever . . . revealing our science to you. I would sooner fall off a seventy story building.' She glanced at Harry Fowler who acknowledged with an encouraging smile.

'Hell let's just calm down here,' protested the President, giving Philby a hard stare, 'nobody's issuing threats against you, your friends or family. We're simply pointing out the facts. Other folks will be pursuing you for this information and they may do so in less pleasant ways.'

'Then we will deal with it in our own way,' said Lucy.

Chu had been expecting this outburst from the outset and had pulled his smart phone out of his pocket and switched it on, ready to flee if necessary. Harry Fowler noticed this and remarked gently, 'Relax Mr Chu, we understand your position totally. You've made it very clear, and I personally guarantee, you will not be threatened or intimidated by the US Government. However there can be no such guarantees for other governments and so I would like to make a suggestion sir. We will provide you with protection from such interference twenty four seven. You will not even know we are there but you will be able to get on with your normal lives until such time as you see fit to help us. If the President agrees I would like to carry out that duty personally. How does that sound?'

Lucy looked at Harry curiously, sensing there was more to this offer than he was actually saying. Harry smiled at her and she softened momentarily.

'We could try it out for a while and see how it goes. What do you think Father?'

Chu shrugged. 'We protect ourselves anyway, but if you think will help, then yes, I agree. I remind you Mr President, Albert Grossman not the only one who can put ICBM's in your back yard.' He deliberately looked around the oval office, as though assessing if a Minuteman missile would fit in the space.

'That's a deal then,' said the President showing a politician's face but internally boiling with frustration and anger.

They shook hands on the deal and Lucy and her father left. The President's fury was directed at Alan Philby after they had gone. 'We had 'em almost on the hook Ira then you have to start threatening and stuff, what sort of negotiatin' stance was that? Ain't you been to no lessons on how to do this sort of stuff? It seems to me this young woman's achieved more on her own than the CIA and FBI put together. Why do I pay you Ira, when you come up with less than nothing? Where were you when this Grossman guy was invading the ISS and dumping three world leaders on there, hey Ira? Where were you and your over-inflated specialist cronies, when our lives were being threatened? It took a slip of a girl to outsmart the lot of you and rescue me. Ira your no use to me, you're fired!'

CHAPTER 25

Lucy and Chu had a very successful day out at Chester Zoo. The research department had become very excited when Chu presented them with their latest acquisition. A Chinese giant salamander was interesting anyway, but one with blue eyes and eyelids, replacing the normal bead like protuberances high up on the broad, flat head, was unique, and sure to boost visitor numbers. And bright pink! Where did this outrageous beast come from?

'Where did you get this creature?' said the head zookeeper, 'It's out of this world.'

'Yes, you almost right,' said Chu, as two of the zoo staff carried the creature into an amphibian enclosure.

'You will feed him properly?' said Lucy gleefully, 'He likes steak, medium, with pepper sauce, but I guess live frogs will be a good enough substitute.'

The despairing human eye fixed on Lucy in appealing fashion, aware that his only hope was her ability to reconstitute the DNA she had so expertly disrupted. She stared at the eye for some moments and detected a flash of hope, then deliberately ignored it.

'Let me see now,' she said turning to the head zookeeper, 'these animals can live for up to fifty years in captivity, can't they?'

He nodded vigorously. 'They certainly can, perhaps we should try and find a mate for him.'

'Oh I wouldn't do that,' she said grinning, 'he prefers the solitary life. He needs time to think about his future without distractions . . . and his past. Perhaps you could install a mirror in there. He's a bit vain you see.'

'Think? You believe he can think?'

'Oh yes! It wouldn't be any fun if he couldn't.'

Perplexed, the zookeeper threw a couple of dead fish into the enclosure and the salamander hoovered them up in its powerful jaws.

'You seem to think it's almost human,' said the zookeeper. 'I suppose you have a pet name for him?'

'Yes,' said Lucy. 'Grossmander, or Gross for short.' She abruptly turned on her heel and walked away.

Chu quickly caught up with her. 'I didn't know you had heart of stone daughter,' he said reprovingly. 'When will you release him?'

She stared at him in surprise. 'I will *never* do that and I want you to promise that you will not interfere,' she answered angrily.

'It saddens me to see you so full of hate,' said Chu. 'This is against the teachings of the Buddha.'

'I am aware of that father, and I have struggled to justify it to myself. I pursue my beliefs as an individual and ask no one else to accept responsibility for them. The Buddha's teaching could not foresee the requirements of the twenty first century and the possibility that one man could inflict so much misery on so many. In these extreme circumstances the vast majority of people are innocent and if possible should be protected from this tyranny. To do this I believe extreme means can be justified. If I took no action although I have it in my power to do this, I would be abdicating my responsibilities to my fellow human beings and hiding behind my beliefs to justify my inaction. This is my personal ambivalence and I ask no one else to share it with me. I may not like it, but regrettably, it is something I must do. Remember Father I have not killed this man, only imprisoned him, in much the same way Jerome was imprisoned . . . by yourself. He killed my mother . . . and me . . . twice!'

'Ah! Yes,' said Chu, 'I must speak with you about that. I have surprise for you, there's someone for you to meet.'

'Oh! Who?'

'It's a surprise.'

'Here at the zoo?'

'Yes, we go have coffee first.'

They made their way to the café, sat at a vacant table and ordered three coffees. Intrigued, Lucy impatiently demanded to know who they were meeting.

'Close your eyes,' said Chu, smiling.

Lucy obeyed and covered her eyes with her hands.

'Ok! You look now,' he said.

She uncovered her eyes and almost fainted with joy as her mother rushed forward to greet her. Chu smiled with pleasure at their emotional re-union.

'How did you do this?' said Lucy through tears of joy.

'I suppose I'm just old romantic,' he said fishing a lock of Carla's hair out of his pocket. 'I've kept this ever since divorce. DNA from hair all I needed to reconstitute Carla. Now we back together again and going to live in Liverpool, in China town, and thanks to you, with blessing of British government.'

Lucy threw her arms around both her parents and hugged them fiercely together. 'This makes me so happy, so very happy. Promise me you will stay together this time?'

Carla kissed her daughter on the cheek. 'Bambina,' she said gently, 'I have been a fool. I didn't recognise what kind of a man I had in your father. I promise I won't give him up ever again.'

Suddenly Lucy realised that she had the opportunity to lay Albert's ghost once and for all. 'Mama you must come and see Albert,' she cried excitedly.

Carla glanced at Chu for guidance and he shook his head. 'Oh Lucia! Is he here? I don't think so,' she said doubtfully.

'But Mama you must see how we have got revenge for the way he treated us.'

'Revenge? What do you mean?'

'Don't worry Mama, he can't hurt us any more. I have seen to that, which is why it is important for you to see for yourself.'

'Oh very well, if you insist,' said Carla, reluctantly.

Lucy and Carla walked back to the amphibian display house hand in hand, chatting excitedly, while Chu looked on wearing a contented smile. They stopped at one of the windows.

'He's here?' said Carla, looking around expectantly, with a worried frown. Lucy pointed to a rock in the middle of the pool where the giant salamander was squatting with its eyes closed.

'That's Albert?' cried Carla. 'Mama mia, you pulla my leg Lucia.'

'No Mama it's true.'

Albert recognised their voices and opened his eyes. Carla caught her breath in horror. 'Mon Dio! It is true! I would recognise those eyes anywhere. How did you do this?'

'That doesn't matter Mama. We are safe as long as I choose to keep him here.'

'But this is an abomination, so very cruel darling, you cannot do this?'

Albert's pleading eyes desperately registered their agreement.

Lucy's jaw set in a determined fashion. 'Mama, the worst moment of my life was when this abomination, your so called protector, held a knife to your innocent neck and caused your blood to flow. I vowed then that I would deliver him to justice . . . my kind of justice. If I were to hand him over to the police he would literally get away with murder, because there are no bodies. He would also try to kill me again, because he knows I can stop any evil plan he's likely to concoct. He has brought this upon himself and my conscience is absolutely clear. Now you have seen him, you have my word he will never trouble us again and that . . . is my final decision.'

The blue eyes closed tight shut, there was no way out!

. . . .

Jack walked into his old room in college and was confronted by Sophie lying on his bed crying as if her world had come to an end. He sat on the bed beside her and put a gentle hand on her shoulder.

'What's the matter?' he said.

She turned from the pillow she was holding and buried her tear stained face in his shoulder for several minutes before speaking. 'Lucy,' she gasped, 'Lucy's turned Albert into a lizard.'

'What? How do you know this?'

'I saw her do it,' she sobbed.

Jack could see she was too upset to pursue the enquiry any further and decided to ask Lucy about it when she returned. He made to stand up, but she pulled him back down to her and hugged him tightly. The warmth of her body against his caused a whirl of sensations he had never known before. Suddenly he was gripped by fear . . . fear of being possessed, and jumped smartly to his feet. Sophie's tearful face gazed up at him. He knew if he gave in he would be lost.

'W . . . we must return you to your previous life,' he stammered, deliberately avoiding her appealing eyes.

'But you must be afraid that I may give away your secrets?'

'Would you? Why would you? What could you gain from it? No one would believe it anyway. Sometimes I even have doubts about it myself,' said Jack. He was aware that Lucy may want to erase her memory, because it was the obvious solution.

'There's nothing there for me anymore, except loneliness now that Albert's gone,' she said mournfully. 'I'm afraid of what Lucy may do to me. I don't want to be a lizard Jack!'

'Oh Sophie! Lucy's not going to harm you. You have my word on that. But you had a life before all this happened. Don't you have a business, an escort agency, providing companionship for tired business men?'

'It's nothing more than high class prostitution. It's not something I want to go back to.'

Jack remembered the problem he had managed to push to the back of his mind for a year. This was the other side of the story. His father's secret life was helping to maintain people like Sophie who hated what they were doing but would otherwise be destitute. Somehow he felt responsible but was at a loss to know how to help her and slumped down on a chair, depression suddenly weighing down on him. It was never a requirement of their exclusive club to accumulate waifs and strays, even attractive ones like Sophie. And then there was Dipper. He, Megan and Lucy would have to have some serious discussions about this. *A Lizard? What has she been up to?*

Lucy appeared with a triumphant smile. Jack felt the back of his neck; this wasn't going to be easy. Sophie took a sip of the coffee Jack had just made for her and looked at Lucy apprehensively. Lucy sensed there was some sort of strained atmosphere and tried to relieve it by describing the events on the ISS and in the oval office afterwards.

She concluded by saying, 'Sophie was brilliant Jack, she was able to distract Albert while I swapped the memory chip in his phone.'

'You turned him into a lizard?' said Jack incredulously.

'Sure, why not? And yesterday my father and I installed him in his new home, in Chester Zoo, where everybody can watch him suffer for the rest of his miserable existence. And guess what?' she said excitedly, 'Father has reconstituted Mama. She's alive and well Jack!' She took hold of Jack's hands and did a little jig around the room.

'That's wonderful news,' said Jack, feeling some responsibility slip from his shoulders. 'How did he do that?'

'He'd kept a lock of Mama's hair. Isn't that romantic?'

Jack stared at her in disbelief.

'What?' she said, with a questioning look.

'Nothing really,' he said, 'I'm just surprised that you consider something . . . anything . . . to be romantic.'

'You really don't know me at all do you Jack Dawkins, even after all we've been through, you still don't know me.'

Jack sighed. 'No! And I don't suppose I ever will. But we need to talk about Sophie and her future.'

'Ah! I see,' said Lucy nodding her head in sudden understanding. 'Sophie's situation brought back memories of your father and his involvement with the corruption of young women like her. You think I'm going to pack her back off to Amsterdam to the miserable existence of a high class street walker, don't you?'

Jack was flabbergasted. 'How do you know all this?'

'You see what I mean, you still don't understand me. You've jokingly called me a witch in the past.'

Jack nodded, 'but . . .'

'You were closer to the truth than you know,' she smiled. 'But I am a white witch . . . not the other kind. OK, so I've changed Albert into a lizard, but that was no more than he deserved and I had to do it to protect everybody else. Even Father was surprised by that. But you see Father's a softy and would allow people to take advantage of him. I will never do that.'

'So what are you going to do about Sophie?'

'OK, I have a suggestion. My parents are getting back together and are going to stay in Liverpool. Father is going to work at the university. I've suggested to them that they are going to need a housekeeper and companion for Mama when Father is away lecturing. Mama doesn't know anyone in Chinatown where they will be living, and spending too much time on her own is what helped to sabotage their marriage before. I think Sophie would be ideal for the job . . . if she wants it of course.'

'But she doesn't have a passport or work permit,' he protested.

'Oh Jack, you should know better by now than to believe that something like that is a problem to me,' she said with a wicked smile. 'Remember I once hacked into your bank account and rearranged it . . . slightly?'

Jack nodded dumbly, *Albert didn't stand a chance,* he thought.

'Well then what do you think?'

'I think you'd better ask Sophie,' said Jack. 'They did share the same bloke for a while . . . they may not get on.'

Lucy turned to Sophie. 'Do you think you could be a companion for my mother?' she asked.

Sophie's face lit up with excitement. 'We do have some things in common and I have no feelings for Albert any more. I think I would like to speak with her first, but yes I would like to try it. I have no reason to go back to Amsterdam. I will speak with my brother and make sure he's alright and has enough money.'

'Good that's settled then, we'll give it a try,' said Lucy.

'And Dipper?' said Jack hesitantly.

'Oh, that's easy,' laughed Lucy. 'He seems to have been adopted by Father. It would appear that I have a brother!'

CHAPTER 26

———— •◦• ————

Christmas day was very special. They had all gathered together at Chu's house which he had rented in the Chinese quarter of Liverpool, and Carla had promised a typically Italian Christmas dinner.

Jack was startled to see the change in his friend Dipper, who seemed to have shed a great deal of weight and his bottle glass spectacles. 'So where did this new svelte you come from?' he said.

'Ah! said Dipper, 'I would like to be able to say from strict dieting, however . . .'

'. . . Chu's been trying out cosmetic surgery,' finished Jack.

'Well, not just that, old chap, he's cured my limp as well.'

'Fantastic!' said Jack. 'And the goggles?'

'Nothing so grand there I'm afraid; contact lenses,' he said slapping Jack on the back.

'Goodness, you look almost human,' said Jack.

'Ah! I've seen the error of my ways,' he said, his eyes following Sophie around the spacious dining room as she busied herself laying the table.

Jack noticed his fascination. 'There wouldn't be some other contributing factors then would there?' he said, in teasing tones.

'Jack, did I ever give you a hard time over any love interest you may have entertained?'

'Yes!' replied Jack, grinning.

'Well, if I did it must have been friendly advice.'

Megan screwed up her nose. '*You* gave Jack advice on affairs of the heart?'

'Certainly!' said Dipper, 'There were times when he needed some counselling from a good friend.'

'You mean interference from a nosey parker,' laughed Megan.

Lucy and Chu walked in to the room to the accompaniment of loud cheers and clapping.

'How do we address someone who regularly rubs shoulders with world leaders?' cried Jack, 'Your Grace or Ma'am?'

'Oh Jack do behave, it just sort of happened. It was never my intention to get cosy with politicians. They just happened to need rescuing from the clutches of an evil arch villain intent on world domination,' she smiled coyly. 'In those circumstances how could I refuse?' She made a dismissive gesture at Jack as if to say it was just an everyday occurrence.

'And then you just happened to drop in on the President of the U.S.A. for burger and chips in the oval office,' laughed Jack. 'He should have realised then that the way to your heart is through your stomach.'

'Yes he got it all wrong,' said Lucy. 'He made the mistake of offering me everything I didn't want . . . or need.'

'And a simple plate of fries would've done the trick,' chortled Jack.

'Second to the code for our computer programmes, that needs to be our best kept secret,' laughed Lucy.

Chu invited them all to be seated at the dining room table and he sat at the head.

'Ladies and Gentlemen,' he said, his face wreathed in smiles. 'I make small speech to celebrate coming together of my new family at this time of year when families . . . ah . . . are important. We are a unique family, with unique talents brought together by "La forza del destino".' He smiled at Carla at this brief foray into Italian. 'We are bonded together, possibly for all time, by common knowledge and purpose. This gives us strength, but mostly our strength lies in our loyalty to each other.' He raised his glass and gave a toast, 'To loyalty!'

After the traditional response Chu introduced Crip and Dunnit, now cured of their virus, who, with Dunnit's baritone and Crip's squeaky falsetto performed the twelve days of Christmas in the centre of the table. This caused much mirth, Crip finding it impossible to get his pronunciation skills around "partridge in a pear tree" and "lords a leaping."

Sophie, clearly upset, left the table and fled into the kitchen quickly followed by Carla where this time, she shed tears of joy. Carla hugged her and caressed her blond hair gently. 'There now, what's the problem?' she said.

'I had forgotten what it was like to have a family,' smiled Sophie, with tears still rolling down her face, 'I'm so happy.'

'Oh darling bambina,' said Carla, 'we have all made mistakes in the past but that is all behind us now. We will make a fresh start. We all have a new family now.'

Carla led her back into the dining room where Lucy had emerged from a bedroom dressed as "La Befana", the

Italian good witch of Christmas. She had a broomstick, false hooked nose and a bag of coal to hand out to the boys and girls who had been naughty through the year.

'Very appropriate,' cheered Jack. 'Now we see you for what you really are.'

To the accompaniment of much amusement, Jack was presented with most of the coal, while everyone else received a small present. The new family then sat at the table and pulled crackers. Lucy whooped in delight at the joke in hers, 'Hey! Listen to this,' she cried, 'why should you invite a salamander to your Christmas party?'

'Because he'll never be legless!' everyone chorused.

'Oh I see,' she said, 'it was a set up.'

'Possibly,' laughed Jack.

Carla and Sophie came out of the kitchen carrying plates of steaming pasta, calamari, tortellini, chicken and beef and placed them on the table.

Then Father Christmas burst into the room, carrying a machine pistol fitted with a silencer!

. . . .

D.S. Collins was shaken out of his daydream by the telephone's urgent trilling.

'Collins!' barked Smiley, 'My office, now!'

He knocked hesitantly at her door.

'Enter!' she bawled.

He shuffled in and stood rigidly to attention staring straight ahead, like a soldier on parade, while his stomach felt like it was doing handstands. Her foul mood washed over him leaving him in no doubt that this interview meant trouble. He risked a glance down at her stony face and glittering, ice like, eyes. *Oh God! What have I done?*

'I have received a package this morning from your colleague in Holland, detective Van Penn,' she said, pronouncing each word deliberately, as though talking to a child. 'It seems that he succeeded where *you* singularly failed.'

She pushed the brown envelope across the desk. Collins already knew what was in it and he felt a shudder run up his spine. *Limp fisted sod! He's dropped me in it.*

'Open it,' instructed Smiley.

Collins took a deep breath, leaned over and tugged the envelope open. The charred remains of the police file on Lucy Chu and her father, slid out onto the desk, spraying soot and charcoal as it went. 'Sorry Ma'am,' he said brushing away the mess with the sleeve of his pristine, white shirt.

'So how did the Dutch police force carry out my specific instructions when you couldn't?'

'Well,' he said, rapidly gathering his thoughts, 'It looks as though it may have been in the flat that caught fire in The Hague Ma'am, and the Dutch police had exclusive access to that.'

'Mm,' said Smiley temporarily caught off balance. 'Why didn't Van Penn tell you about this before?'

'Regrettably Ma'am, Mr Van Penn and I did not have, let's say . . . the best of relationships.'

'Damn it man you're both professionals, you should have been able to rise above that sort of school yard nonsense.'

'Yes Ma'am,' said Collins meekly.

She pulled out a manila folder from her desk drawer. 'Right,' she growled, 'here's your report. It looks as though you went to Holland for a couple of day's holiday. It's almost as sparse as the ideas in your head.'

Collins gulped. 'I thought it was a straightforward accident Ma'am. I left it for the Dutch police to deal with.'

'Oh yes Collins, the Dutch police.' She pulled out a much thicker folder. 'This is a copy of their report. It reads like something out of "Alice in Wonderland".' She tapped the folder with one unpainted finger nail. 'Where were you when all this was going on?'

So much for our agreement; the little rat, thought Collins. 'Mr Van Penn is blessed with a highly developed imagination,' he offered.

Smiley peered up at him incredulously. 'And did Mr Van Penn imagine that the two corpses found in the burnt out flat have disappeared from the mortuary?'

'Disappeared Ma'am?'

'Yes Collins, disappeared . . . pouf! But they didn't walk out, and I do believe there is no call for body snatchers anymore, even in Holland. So how did this occur?'

'I . . . I . . . didn't know . . .'

'You don't know very much do you, about what's going on under your very nose?'

'No Ma'am.'

'Mr Albert Grossman, where is he?'

'I don't know Ma'am.'

'While you were no doubt enjoying the dubious delights of Amsterdam's red light district, I can tell you that your Mr Grossman illegally took over a major oil company in Houston, survived an assassination attack by the CIA, transported an ICBM into CIA headquarters and kidnapped three world leaders to the International Space Station. He then exploded a nuclear device in China, presented a major threat to world peace and was finally rendered harmless by . . . Lucy Chu, whose corpse has disappeared from a Dutch morgue. You knew nothing about any of this?'

Collins's mind went blank. 'But Lucy Chu's dead Ma'am,' he offered feebly.

'However much you repeat it Collins, it still sounds like a very lame excuse for your inadequacy. Even my poor desk bound brain can see the flaw in that argument. She cannot be dead Collins. She is very much alive. The only thing resembling dead meat is that which resides between your ears. If she were dead why would the President of the United States of America be conferring upon her, "The Presidential Medal of honour"; the Russian President, "The Hero of the Russian Federation Award", and the Chinese Premier, "The Order of Dr Sun Yat-Sen"? None of these awards are being presented posthumously. So if the three leading nations on this planet think she's alive, why do you disagree?'

Collins suddenly had a flashback to his previous boss, Livingstone, and his mental state after Lucy Chu had disappeared from custody at Heathrow airport. His mouth kept opening and closing clearly expecting a supply of words to justify its inane activity, but his mind had been consumed in an overload fog of unbelievable information.

Suddenly Smiley became more businesslike as she decided there was little point in chopping any more lumps off the desolate Collins. 'Assuming you know where it is, get yourself down to the Thames,' she said abruptly. 'Talk to the river police who have just fished out a stiff. I want you to go and have a look.'

'Anything particular about this one?' said Collins tentatively, relieved at the change of subject.

'Yes,' she said, 'his name is Grossman, Jon Grossman. He's Dutch but has been working in this country for some years as a lorry driver. His lorry is parked in a lay by on the A1 just north of the city.'

'Phew!' whistled Collins noiselessly. 'Do you think he may be related to Albert Grossman?'

Smiley stared at him in disbelief. 'I'll let you draw your own conclusions when you've seen the body. Apparently he's been whipped to death! Oh! And you may have to involve your bosom friend, Mr Van Penn. Go on, get out!' snapped Smiley at the open mouthed Collins, 'I'll deal with you later when your faculties have returned.'

Collins groaned inwardly and left.

CHAPTER 27

———— •●• ————

At first everyone thought it was a joke. They realised their error when they heard the menace in the man's voice. 'Don't anybody move!'

Lucy recognised the American accent immediately. 'Mr Philby,' she said, 'how kind of you to drop in. Happy Christmas!'

Jack, sensing the danger, ran his mental programme and promptly disappeared from the table.

'Get him back now!' shouted Philby, pointing the gun at Lucy, 'Or she dies.'

There was a short pause then Jack reappeared.

'That's better,' said Philby. He waved the gun at Lucy and pushed a piece of paper and a pen in front of Chu. 'Put your smart phones on the table,' he snapped. Jack, Lucy and Chu slid their phones into the middle of the table where Philby could plainly see them. 'Now,' he continued, putting Lucy's phone in his pocket, 'write down the password for the programme, then I will leave you and you can play happy families again.'

'Don't do it Chu,' cried Megan. 'I can see what he has in his mind. He's going to kill us all anyway.'

'Ah! The mind reading minx,' growled Philby, with a harsh cough. 'Now I understand. So you can read minds eh?' He pointed the gun at Megan's head. 'The next mind you read will be your last . . . is that clear?' Megan nodded dumbly. Chu calmly took the piece of paper, wrote something on it and pushed it across the table to Philby who folded it roughly and pushed it in his pocket.

'Regrettably,' said Philby, 'I have to wipe you all out together to prevent you regenerating each other. Any one of you left alive could interfere with my plans. I'm afraid it's the only way . . . I am so very sorry,' he said mockingly.

'How you know I give you correct . . . ah . . . password?' said Chu, with an innocent smile.

Philby glared at him. 'If this password is not correct, I will kill all of you,' he cried, doubt and desperation in his voice.

'And then?' said Chu. 'You going to do that anyway, so we have nothing to lose, but you lose everything. We cannot give password if all dead!'

Philby glared at Lucy venomously. 'Maybe! But I will have the satisfaction of knowing I have my revenge on the one who caused me to lose my job.'

With a shaking hand, he retrieved the paper from his pocket and tried to read what Chu had written. 'This is all in Chinese,' he snarled, passing the paper to Lucy. 'What does it say?'

Lucy choked in a fit of giggles as she read what Chu had written.

'What does it say?' shouted Philby, his face purple with rage.

'"Those who know do not speak, those who speak, do not know,"' she read.

'Don't play your mystical games with me. If you don't give me the key to your programme I will shoot you all, one by one, starting with her,' he screamed. He pointed the weapon at the terrified Sophie, the finger pressure on the trigger increasing visibly. Suddenly, Dipper flung himself at Philby and attempted to wrestle the gun from his hand, while Sophie instinctively threw herself on the floor. The gun went off with a loud plop and Dipper slumped forward almost knocking Philby off balance. Philby stepped back smartly and continued to wave the gun menacingly at the group while Dipper crashed to the floor, bleeding from a chest wound. Sophie cried out in anguish and tried to resuscitate the dying Dipper. Carla rushed to the table and grabbed Chu's smart phone to call for help but Philby knocked it out of her hand.

'Not necessary dear,' said Chu calmly, pointing at Jack, 'we have our own doctor.' Jack nodded his understanding and promptly disappeared once more. Sophie let out a surprised cry as Dipper also vanished.

Confronted by the now grinning Chinaman, Philby panicked as he realised that as fast as he shot his captives they would be regenerated by Jack. His eyes, wild and staring over the false beard, flickered from side to side in desperation as he tried to think of a way in which he could regain the initiative. 'Who's next?' he screamed, 'One by one, until somebody gives me the correct code!' He pointed the gun at Megan's head.

Chu glanced at the wall mirror behind Philby's head. There was the sound of a sharp crack of a gunshot and the window behind Chu shattered. Everyone except Chu assumed Philby's pistol had gone off again and dived for cover under the table. Chu remained seated, impassively watching the figure outside the window behind him, in the mirror's reflection. Philby swayed slightly. The hole which had appeared in his forehead began to well fresh blood. His legs buckled underneath him and he collapsed onto the table, his head buried in a plate of tortellini. The Santa hood fell forward to hide the mess and the gun clattered harmlessly to the floor. The door swung open and Harry Fowler strode in purposefully, carrying a sniper's rifle. 'It's all right,' Lucy shouted to everyone, 'he's one of ours.' She slumped in a chair and began to cry with relief. Seeing that Lucy was upset Fowler went straight over to her and took her in his arms to comfort her.

'Are you all right?' he murmured softly.

'No!' she wailed.

'Where are you hurt?' said Harry, becoming alarmed.

'I'm not hurt,' she sobbed.

'So why are you crying?'

Mischievously, she snuggled closer to him, tilted her tear stained face up towards him and pouted alluringly. 'You've ruined the tortellini . . . my favourite Italian food,' she complained.

Dipper materialised along with Jack and beamed at the astonished Sophie. She ran to him, threw her arms around his neck and kissed him. 'Is it really you?' she cried, 'You were dead a few minutes ago!'

'I don't understand it myself. I remember the gun going off and then nothing. I think Jack must have worked a miracle to save me.'

Jack acknowledged with a thumbs up sign. 'That's what friends are for,' he grinned, 'just don't play the hero in future when I'm not around.'

'Well! Who would have thought it,' said Megan admiringly. 'The overstuffed loathsome caterpillar has become a beautiful butterfly. A slimmed down bloody super hero, so he is, and almost handsome with it too!'

'Hey!' said Sophie, tearfully, 'Lay off him taffy, he's *my* hero.'

'Don't worry,' said Megan waspishly, 'some things haven't changed. I expect he's still a nosey parker.'

Chu rose from the table and went to greet and thank Harry Fowler for his intervention. 'You right, some things we cannot do, some things you can . . . but we don't normally leave litter,' he said, indicating the corpse sprawled on the table.

'Point taken,' grinned Harry. 'Will someone give me a hand to take this trash out?'

Dipper and Jack helped carry the ex deputy CIA director outside while Carla and Sophie cleared the mess on the table and revitalized Christmas dinner as best they could. Harry Fowler joined them in their resumed celebrations at the table and was introduced to members of the group he had not previously met as a US Government protection officer. 'I just need to get the garbage collection organised,' he said, pulling out his mobile phone.

Carla raised her eyebrows. 'On Christmas day?' she cried.

'We get special rates for traitors,' smiled Harry, grimly.

'But why?' said Lucy, 'Why did he do this?'

'After you left, the President sacked him on the spot for trying to bully you. I guess it tipped him over the edge. We followed his movements closely after that. This wasn't unexpected.' He pointed at Dipper. 'Say, if you can be brought back from the dead, does this mean you're all immortal?'

Chu grinned at him and put his arm affectionately around Carla's waist. 'No one in this family will . . . ah . . .

outlive their usefulness,' he said enigmatically. Carla smiled and gently nodded her agreement.

'Just a moment,' smiled Lucy, 'hold that call, I need to send your President a Christmas present.'

Harry gazed at her in astonishment. 'You do?' he said lamely.

'Certainly, a reminder of our brief relationship, a little keepsake if you like,' and she disappeared outside.

She re-emerged a little while later wearing a big smile and carrying a bullet, which she handed to Harry. He turned it over in his fingers and examined the minute inscription etched on its surface. 'CIA Deputy Director Alan Philby, R.I.B.,' he read. The questioning look in his eyes made her giggle.

'R.I.B.?' he said, with a puzzled frown.

'Yes, "Rest In Bullet". That's Philby,' she laughed. 'You don't need to call your garbage disposal team. I've collapsed his material self into the bullet that killed him!'

'But how?' spluttered the astounded American.

'Let's just say that for a modern sorceress it's not a difficult thing to do. What I've done to Philby I can do to anyone, including Rick Newman. After all I do have his DNA,' she said with a mischievous look. 'Give him that with my regards. He can keep it on his desk as a memento, or if his ego ever needs a boost, he can fire Philby again can't he?'

Harry Fowler shook his head slowly. *Will I ever understand the nature of Lucy Chu. This twenty first century Buddhist witch, seems to have put a spell on me,* he thought. *She doesn't seem to take anything seriously. How the hell am I going to keep this will o' the wisp from harm when she can just disappear to God knows where in the blink of an eye?*

As if realising his dilemma, Lucy took him by the arm and pulled him close to her. She gazed seriously up into his eyes and whispered, 'Don't worry darling, I'll look after you!'